That First Heady Burn

In This Series

That First Heady Burn

True Vermilion

The Dark Shill

A Stack of Sawbucks

The Hillside Roble

The Peroxide Pomp

The Incidental Twin

Brawl in Bardo

The Window-Shade Job

The Convenient Patsy

The Artisanal Grifter

Shrink in the Shadows

Project Chartreuse

From a Desert Playa

The Tired Canary

A Desperate Frame-up

Trail of the Blue Agave

The Saucer-Heads

That First Heady Burn

That First Heady Burn

George Bixley

DAGMAR MIURA
LOS ANGELES

Published by Dagmar Miura
Los Angeles
www.dagmarmiura.com

That First Heady Burn

This is a work of fiction. Names, characters, businesses, places, events, and incidents are either the products of the author's imagination or used in a fictitious manner. Any resemblance to actual persons, living or dead, or actual events is purely coincidental.

First published 2017

ISBN: 978-1-942267-44-7

ONE

H E JUST HAD one of those faces, this guy, that needed to be punched, and Slater imagined how satisfying it would feel to do that—not just punching him, but putting his fist right through it. Slater slid farther down behind the steering wheel as the guy turned toward him, and kept him centered in his binoculars. His target hadn't noticed him, Slater decided, parked down the block in a dark spot between streetlights in the black Thunderbird. The guy was just restless, looking around.

Insurance fraud was Slater's gig—uncovering it, by surveilling people like Punch-face all over Los Angeles. On these operations he usually waited until the target's windows went dark before he called it quits, but in a stroke of luck the guy had come out of his apartment, which was perched over a two-car garage next to someone else's house, and lurched down the flight of stairs to the street, to smoke, it seemed, the glowing red dot of a cigarette in one hand, a Corona in the other.

The target lingered at the bottom of the stairs, then strolled to the other side of the garage door, next to the hedge of bougainvillea, the deep-pink petals visible even in the low light. Ignoring the shrubbery, he took a deep drag, and then a swig from the bottle dangling from his other hand. He didn't seem to be limping, even though he was wearing a tightly bound black brace on his left knee, and he certainly wasn't hobbled like he had been at the face-to-face last week in the insurance company's conference room. Slater got invited to those when the bean-counters were suspicious of their claimants, and they usually didn't hire him unless there was something blatantly hinky going on.

Punch-face had made an on-the-job injury claim, his knee twisted in a fall at the tech-parts warehouse he worked at in east LA County. "Not East LA," the tech company representative had admonished them all at the meeting. "We're in the unincorporated eastern part of the county." Slater had wanted to punch the shit-eating smile off that guy's face too. Realistically, though, if he did things like that, he'd never get jobs.

The target took a long last drag and dropped his butt, grinding it into the sidewalk—with his right foot, not the side he'd injured—and walked back toward the stairs. From the neck down he actually wasn't unattractive, his athletic legs on full display tonight under his baggy boxer shorts. Yeah, he'd fuck him, Slater decided, as long as he didn't have to listen to that whiny voice again, or look him in the eye. The guy sank onto the bottom step, gripping the handrail to lower himself, as if his knee really did hurt. Sipping beer, he sat there, staring at nothing. It was hot out, and if he didn't have air-conditioning in that little apartment, the street would be the most comfortable place to be on a muggy August night.

Slater sighed and set down the binoculars, rubbing his eyes. What was this punk's name? Something with a *J;* Joshua, or Justin. He hesitated to turn on his tablet, as the glow of its screen would ruin his night vision, but he did it anyway. Jason Hughes, that was it, he saw, scrolling through his documentation. Not even thirty yet. If that injury was real, he didn't envy Jason—he'd be dealing with it the rest of his life. Slater scrawled a few lines at the bottom of his notes:

12:40 a.m. Smoke break. Wearing knee brace. Limp: undetermined.

A loud *thump* broke the quiet of the night, and Slater dropped the tablet and instinctively ducked his head. It was Jason, looming over the car, his face contorted in anger. He slapped his palm on the windshield again.

"You're Ibáñez, right?" he demanded. "Working for the insurance company?"

Slater rolled down his window a few inches and looked up at him. "You're tight, brother. You might fall and hurt yourself again. Go on home."

"Or what?" he demanded.

"Or I'll rip your balls off and shove them down your fucking throat."

Jason stepped back, not reacting, his eyes dulled by the drink. "Big talk. Go home yourself, grease ball."

Slater was dark, with Latin features, and had jet-black hair, but this was nothing but a slur, and absurd because Jason wore his own hair in a long unctuous ponytail. But then, racism wasn't rational.

He jumped out of the Thunderbird, leaving the door open, and strode after Jason, determination in his gait. Slater was tall, over six feet, and thick, and combined with Jason's inebriation, it made him easy to manipulate. Grabbing his wrist, he twisted him around, shoving his shoulder down, the Corona bottle dropping to the asphalt and smashing into a puddle of glass shards and foamy beer.

"Ow," Jason protested, slapping at Slater's jeans with his other hand, but Slater grabbed that wrist too and forced his hand to the top of his head, rubbing it on Slater's hair.

"Is that greasy? I had a shower today, punk, did you?"

He let Jason twist out of his grip and stumble away, climbing the stairs toward his front door, forgetting about his limp, looking back at Slater with wide eyes. That look—they always had that look, an amalgam of anger and fear.

Slater moved the Thunderbird a couple of blocks and parked again. Done with Jason for the night, he pulled out his cell phone and thumbed through his hookup app. It was getting late, but there were always guys on the hunt. Almost right away someone winked at him, using the handle 21Heart, and the guy's profile came up. His head shot was hot, Slater decided, dark-green eyes, a riot of freckles, and untamed African hair, although he did look a little young. But the guy had already done half the work by expressing an interest in Slater. He messaged him:

In my car. Can I swing by or pick you up?

21Heart responded by naming an intersection on Vermont, near USC, just a few minutes' drive from here. It was a little suspicious that he didn't send a street address. Hopefully he was just paranoid about strangers knowing where he lived rather than some closeted frat boy from the dorms. Even worse would be if he were homeless. Those guys always wanted to linger in his apartment, where there was a shower and a warm bed.

When he rolled up on the corner, a skinny kid was standing nearby, hands shoved in his jacket pockets. Standing alone in the dark, he looked even younger than his photo implied.

Slater pulled to the curb and rolled down the passenger window. "21Heart?" he asked.

"Yeah." The kid squatted down, both hands on the window frame, his face innocent, eager. "You're not crazy or dangerous, are you?"

"Both," Slater said flatly. "But not to you."

He grinned and pulled open the door, climbing in. Slater pulled away from the curb, merging into the traffic on Vermont.

"I love the square jaw," the kid said, looking him over. "You're hotter than your picture."

"And you're younger than yours," Slater said, eyeing him. "Please tell me you're not actually twenty-one."

"Why should that matter? You're not that old."

"I can't fuck you," Slater said, keeping his eyes on the road.

"Because I'm too young? Just like that?" He

folded his arms. "Well, that sucks."

"Where do you live?"

"I'm from out of town."

"OK, then where are you staying?"

"With people I meet."

Slater glanced at him again. He didn't seem drug-addled, he decided.

"Swing by the LGBT Youth Center in Hollywood," Slater said. "They can help you find a place to stay that's not dependent on providing sex."

"What's wrong with sex? It's starting to sound like you're against it."

"Not at all—but you shouldn't have to put out to have a place to sleep."

The kid didn't respond, instead looking out the window at the dark city rolling by.

"Where can I drop you?" Slater asked.

"In Hollywood," he said glumly, and named an intersection.

"So where are you from?"

"New Orleans."

"Why would you come out here?"

"Why are you here?" the kid demanded, glaring at him.

Slater sighed and drove in silence. The kid might not even be twenty-one—he still had the temperament of a teenager.

As he pulled up to the curb, the kid popped the door handle.

"Wait," Slater said, and pulled out his wad of cash, finding two hundreds and peeling them off, handing them across.

"I'm not turning tricks," he said, indignant.

"Good," Slater said emphatically, gesturing with the bills. "Don't start."

The kid pocketed the cash, then turned to face him. "Why don't you want me?"

"It's nothing personal. You're a good-looking kid, but I'd feel like a child predator. Fuck people your own age."

After the kid climbed out, Slater pulled away from the curb and headed toward his own neighborhood—gritty and crowded and gang-ridden Westlake. It was hectic and felt like the Third World sometimes, but it was cheap, and central, and where he needed to be. His dingy one-bedroom was two flights above a cell-phone store, but it had its own private garage in the alley out back, with a door on it, and to Slater that was invaluable.

It was too late to mess around finding another guy, so he stopped at a liquor store. Bourbon was almost as good as sex, and if he couldn't have both tonight, he could always have bourbon. In the little parking lot he pulled up beside a police cruiser, its lone uniformed occupant glancing up at him as he parked but then turning back to the glow of her cell phone's screen.

The door chime rang as he stepped inside. Even though the shelves were packed with snacks and soft drinks and beer, any place open this late kept the hard stuff behind the counter, and Slater stepped up to talk to the clerk, a ruddy guy with oily hair and rough skin.

"Jim Beam, black label. Give me three of them." He tapped his phone on the terminal to pay, and waited as the clerk wrapped them each in a paper sack, then put all three in a bag with handles. As he was lifting it off the counter, he heard a jovial voice behind him.

"Hey gumshoe. You're out late."

Slater turned to find a cop in full uniform, his heavy ballistic vest puffing out his chest, his badge shiny in the bright fluorescent light, his weapon conspicuous and holstered at his hip. In one hand he held a couple of cans of caffeinated sugar water. Conrad. Such a good-looking guy, although he hated that stupid cop haircut. Slater never let himself get emotional about guys, as it made him feel weak, but he'd let it happen with this guy, had fallen for him, and after a gut-wrenching attempt at having a relationship, Conrad had unceremoniously dumped him.

Standing here now, that crooked smile on his face just made Slater sneer. "Fuck you, Conrad," he said, and shoved his chest with his palm. Not hard, just enough to make him step back.

Conrad looked surprised, not upset. It was one of the most infuriating things about him, that he was so even-tempered.

"You know you just assaulted a police officer, in view of, like, six security cameras?" Conrad said.

"It's a reflex, when I see trash," Slater said. "Like flicking a mosquito off my arm."

"No fighting in here," the clerk said, raising his voice.

"It's fine," Conrad told him, glancing toward the counter for a second, and then looking back to Slater, his eyes dropping pointedly to the bag hanging from his hand. "Having a little nightcap?"

"You're not my mother," Slater said, suddenly conscious of the weight of the bottles.

"Still, that's a lot of booze."

"It never bothered you when I had my dick down your throat."

Conrad frowned, and cocked his head. "Why are you being so crass?"

Slater stepped closer, jutting his chin out. "Stay the fuck out of my neighborhood, and stay the fuck out of my store." With that, he walked out.

"I can't," Conrad called after him. "It's on my beat."

"It's not your store," the clerk said, raising his voice to be heard over the door chime.

Slater drove home fuming, nosing the Thunderbird into the alley and waiting while the door to his garage rolled up. Trudging up the two flights to his apartment, all he could think about was that first sip. He found a clean glass, dropped a single ice cube into it, and then broke the seal on one of the bottles he'd just carried up, leaving the other two on the kitchen counter in the bag, next to his keys. Just the sound of the bottle opening was enough to start his mind unspooling, his muscles relaxing.

After he poured enough into the glass to get started, he stepped around the island into the living room, really just the other end of the room the kitchen was in, and sat in the dark, sinking into his recliner. The lone window at the end had a view of the lifeless facade of the building across the street, but above that was a strip of empty sky, glowing now with the ambient nighttime light of the metropolis.

Relishing the beautiful burn of the first taste, he felt it in his nostrils, the liquid not yet cold, but heady and familiar, the most reliable lover ever. Why did he have to run into that heartbreaking moron, with his perfect crooked smile? If he wasn't a cop he would have punched that smile right off his face. Conrad. He could still remember how his skin felt, the taste of his sweat, the scent of cedar from the soap he used.

Taking a deeper drink from his glass, he could feel the buzz starting, the calm washing over his body, release.

TWO

WAKING LATE, SLATER lay there for a while, trying to remember how he got onto the bed. He couldn't remember, but his mouth felt dry, and his head was throbbing. He was naked, and he looked around for evidence of how that had happened. His jeans and his boots were in a pile by the closet, his shirt nowhere in sight.

In the bathroom he held up the bottle of ibuprofen and shook some into his mouth, then found a granola bar in the kitchen cupboard and ate it to push the tablets down. Filling a mug with tap water, he spooned instant coffee into it from the container in the fridge, not bothering to microwave it, then sank onto the sofa to drink it and look at his phone.

His head hurt worse when he tried to focus his eyes, but he forced himself to overcome it, and found that he'd missed a call from Della, his handler at the insurance company, Cudahy Mutual. Tapping at the screen to hear the voice message, he winced at the loud beep at the head of the recording, then struggled to turn the volume down.

"I heard you were out late," Della had told the machine. "Swing by my office today when you get a chance."

"Damn it," he said under his breath. Punchface Jason had complained about him.

He got up and stretched his back, rolling his shoulders and flexing his arms, trying to get the blood moving. It made his head throb, but he felt more awake. The bathroom mirror showed his eyes were a little bloodshot, and he splashed water on his face, but he couldn't bring himself to be bothered to shave. In the bedroom he pulled on the jeans from yesterday and found a clean black shirt in the closet.

"Thank you, Rosa," he said, pulling it on. He'd never asked her to do laundry, just clean the place as best she could, but one day she must have decided to take pity on him, or grown tired of his pile of dirty clothes, and eventually he'd started paying her extra for doing it.

After he backed the Thunderbird into the

alley, he waited for the garage door to roll down, then drove the short distance to Cudahy Mutual's offices in downtown LA, just across the chasm of the 110 freeway. In the underground parking lot he tossed the keys to the valet.

"Sweet ride," the guy said. "What year is it?"

"It's a '78," Slater said, pulling his canvas satchel over his shoulder and walking into the elevator lobby.

The receptionist on the thirty-fourth floor wasn't someone he'd seen before, dark-haired and model-thin, wearing red.

"I'm here for Della," he told her.

"I'll see if she's available," the woman said. "If you'll have a seat."

"You don't get to condescend to me," Slater said sharply. "She called me in here. She'd better be fucking available."

A worried look on her face, the woman stood and went down the hall, where he knew Della's office was. A moment later she came back with Della, who grinned when she spotted him.

"Come on back," she said.

In her late fifties, Della didn't stand on cere-mony either, and looped her arm through his as they walked to her office. Today she had her hair sprayed into a kind of helmet, a style that made her look older than she needed to. She still had her hourglass figure, though, the belt on her dress cinched tight to accentuate it.

"You have a bad habit of scaring people," she said, leaning into his shoulder as they walked.

"People have a bad habit of wasting my time. Besides, you pay me to scare people."

She chuckled at that and sat on the sofa at the side of her office, and Slater joined her, dropping into the armchair. It was a small space, but she had a great view out over the city, the tree-studded concrete and asphalt patchwork stretching into the haze at the horizon.

"I'm thinking you got a call from your fraudster," Slater said, setting his satchel at his feet.

Della's eyebrows shot up. "Have you already made that determination?"

"Not yet. I've got my hopes up."

She nodded. "He said you were watching his house."

"Of course I was watching his house. It's what I do."

"He also said you made him touch your hair."

"That's crazy," Slater said. "Who would do that?"

"It did sound odd. He was quite upset, however. Perhaps you could apologize."

"For doing my job? Why would I do that?"

"Because we need to maintain some sense of propriety with our claimants. You don't have to take him candy and flowers, but go easy."

"All right," he said, unable to keep the scowl off his face.

"You might want to talk to him in person again anyway. Something came up." She rose and took a sheaf of paper from her desk, handing it to Slater. "I was digging around in an industry database. It's a record of a previous injury claim."

"So he's a serial fraudster," Slater said, flipping through the pages.

"Maybe. It was several years ago." She waited while Slater scanned the file.

Finally he said, "It doesn't say what the injury was, or how it happened. Why would that be omitted?"

"Insurance companies care about revenues and payouts, not the details. I'm sure Jason Hughes can enlighten you."

Slater slid the paperwork into his satchel, pulling it onto his shoulder as he rose. "I'll stop by there today."

Rising with him, Della said, "Play nice."

"Della—my middle name is discretion."

"That sounds far-fetched. Just try not to man-handle him again."

"I only do that in extreme circumstances, and never without cause."

Della chuckled. "You really know how to make me laugh. It's an attractive quality, Slater. You should let me take you out sometime."

He sighed. "For the tenth time, Della, no dice. But if I magically turn hetero someday, you'll be my first call."

She grinned and put a hand on his shoulder, walking him to her office door. There weren't many people that Slater would let hang on him that way, grabbing his arm and touching his shoulder, but he liked Della, and more importantly, he depended on her for work.

On the way out, by the receptionist's desk, he saw that the woman in red was watching him warily.

"Boo," he said as he passed, and chuckled to himself as he waited for the elevator.

Once he'd recovered his car, he drove back to Hyde Park, pulling up and stopping right at the bottom of Jason's stairs. There was no point in being discreet—Jason had burned him last night, and from now on he'd be wary.

Slater climbed the stairs and banged on Jason's door. Hearing no movement, he pounded again.

"Come on, Jason. You have to talk to me eventually."

This time there was stirring within, then the door opened a few inches.

"It looks like you've sobered up," Slater said. "Can I come in?"

Jason scowled but pulled it open, leading Slater inside, limping to the sofa and then easing himself onto it. Slater watched his movements, trying to decide if they were exaggerated for his benefit, and then took a chair opposite. The place smelled like weed, although Jason didn't look baked.

"I've told you people everything that happened," Jason said, "and I filled out all your forms. What do you want now?"

"I was asked to apologize to you for what happened last night."

His eyebrows shot up. "Really?"

"Yes. So—I'm sorry that you're a racist little fuck."

"I'm not a racist," he snapped.

"You called me a grease ball. I'd call that a racial slur. It's also kind of odd coming from someone who actually has greasy hair."

"I use pomade," Jason said, self-consciously touching his ponytail. "It's a black thing."

Slater raised his eyebrows. "It's interesting that you identify as black. I would have pegged you as a stupid white guy, not a stupid black guy. I guess racism transcends race."

"Did you come here just to insult me," Jason said, angry now, "or is there something you need?"

Slater opened his satchel and pulled out his paperwork. "You gave me everything I needed about the accident when you were in the office the other day, so I'm good on that. What you didn't tell us about was that you made a similar claim eight years ago." He flipped the top page over and scanned the next one. "You were living in Fresno."

"I wasn't living there. Some idiot rear-ended me on the freeway when I was driving through. That claim was for whiplash—it had nothing to do with my job."

That was disappointing, Slater thought, because it sounded legit, and he'd love nothing better than to nail this guy. He asked him a couple of questions about the collision, and Jason even remembered the name of the other driver. Slater added it to his notes on his tablet, then shifted tack.

"What was your relationship like with your employer before the accident?" he asked, watching Jason closely.

"Fine," he said, throwing up his hands. "It's a job, you know? Pack boxes, load trucks."

"Climb ladders," Slater offered.

"Right."

"You reported to the guy who came to that meeting?"

"Preston Goff. I'd talk to him or Karen Chen when I had questions. The work wasn't complicated. All the time-card and payroll stuff was handled by software."

"You didn't actually have a boss?"

Jason shrugged. "I'd get work assignments on

my phone from whoever, and I'd collaborate with the other guy on the shop floor. I guess the software was the boss."

"I've never heard of a company structured that way."

"There was really no one to report to, because there aren't many people working there. Gislitech is shady, bruh, but I keep my head down."

"In what way?"

Jason's eyes grew wide. "Just generally, I guess. I shouldn't have said that."

"But you did say it. How exactly is it shady?"

He shook his head, his mouth tight. "I don't need any more trouble."

Slater shuffled his tablet and the paperwork into his satchel, rising and swinging it over his shoulder. "Someone will be in touch about your claim," he said. "Take care of that knee, if the injury is real."

Jason rose and followed him toward the door. "I should file another complaint about you."

Slater laughed and turned back to face him. "I don't think you realize how this works. One word from me that you're faking your injury, and your claim gets denied. Right now I'm still not convinced one way or the other. I'm basically your only shot at getting paid. So why don't you help yourself out by telling me why you think Gislitech is shady?"

"Why don't you go fuck yourself?" Jason said.

Slater grabbed him by the throat and slammed him against the wall. Jason fought back, clawing at Slater's face, but Slater grabbed one of his wrists.

"Quit it," Slater said, tightening his grip on Jason's throat.

Knowing he was overpowered, Jason stopped, and Slater moved closer, glaring into his panicky eyes. At close range he could smell Jason's musky pomade, and combined with the warm insistent pulsing of Jason's blood under his fingers, it was turning him on. Breathing so hard and flushed with adrenaline, he wondered if Jason would even notice Slater's woody.

"Why is Gislitech shady?" he demanded.

"I can't," Jason whined.

"Who are you afraid of?"

"I'm not supposed to know. They'll come after me."

"Last chance," Slater said, tightening his grip, but Jason just closed his eyes, shook his head.

He let him go, and Jason sank to the floor, gasping for air. There might be more to this than it seemed, Slater thought, closing Jason's door behind him and trotting down the stairs.

Pulling the Thunderbird around the corner, he parked on a long block with those archetypal towering royal palms, old ones, he knew, because they were at least seventy feet tall, and he admired them for a moment, watching the fronds flutter lazily in the breeze. This neighborhood was beautiful in the daytime.

He checked the rearview to make sure Punch-face Jason hadn't followed him, and then dug through his files, looking for details on Gislitech. The smarmy rep who'd come into the office last week, Preston Goff, had the title of director, and there was an address for the company's office. It was the same address where Jason had his injury, he saw, flipping through the pages. It wouldn't take long to drive over to the east part of the county, as distinct from East LA. Traffic wouldn't be bad for another hour.

When he pulled up outside the Gislitech building, he spent a minute looking it over. The neighborhood was only partly industrial, commercial buildings on one side of this street but residential on the other. The structure was old, probably originally office and warehouse space spread over four or five floors. Modern automation meant multiple-floor warehouses weren't very functional, so a lot of these had been converted to office space or live-work lofts. He wasn't sure about this one—the upper-floor windows had old-school glass panes in them, but half of them were walled off from the inside. Just above the first floor, a big yellow-and-black sign announced GISLITECH.

Driving up the block, he parked the Thunderbird well away from the building. Over the years he'd learned never to leave his wheels in view of where he was going. It had seemed counterintuitive at first, but having the car out of sight made it easier to get away in a hurry when he needed to.

Walking back toward Gislitech, he saw that there were security cameras on both corners of the building. Facing the street beside it, providing access to the back, was a reinforced steel gate topped with tidy looping coils of razor wire. It was rolled open today, he saw as he walked by, revealing an empty paved lot stretching behind the building, which was studded with three more cameras trained on the yard. Why did they need such heavy security? The office door, with the street number marked above it, also faced the street, and on either side in two raised beds were birds of paradise, not blooming yet but close to it, their heads dark and swollen. Pulling open the door, he saw a camera a few feet overhead, pointed right at him.

Behind the counter in the lobby sat a woman, maybe in her thirties, with long dark hair and a distractingly crooked nose. Slater realized she was one of the people Jason had mentioned, as her identity was etched into a plastic name plate resting on the counter in front of her: KAREN CHEN. She looked up from her computer screen, disinterested, and asked, "Can I help you?"

"I'm here to see Preston Goff," Slater said, leaning on the counter.

"Can I ask what this is regarding?"

"Insurance fraud. I met with Goff last week, and I'm following up. My name is Slater Ibáñez." He pronounced it the Anglo way, *"ee-bah-nez,"* so she'd retain it.

She rose and mumbled "one moment," then started up the stairs behind her desk.

Slater listened to her heels clicking on the steps, then looked around the lobby. Mid-century, he decided, and it had been restored rather than renovated. No one would redo a building today with those translucent glass blocks on either side of the door, that spatter-pattern flooring; it was all original. The place seemed quiet, considering it was still business hours, with nobody around, no indication that there was any work going on.

Karen clacked down the stairs again and told him, "Follow me."

She led him back up the stairs, into the corridor, and stopped in front of the first doorway, waiting for him to go in and then heading back down.

Goff was wearing a different suit today, chocolate brown with a bright pastel tie, and he rose from behind his desk when he saw Slater. He was a skinny guy, not athletic, and had artificial blond running through his shaggy hair. It was calculated to look unkempt in a very specific way, and Slater knew that was expensive to achieve.

"Mr. Ibáñez," Goff said, grinning affably, meeting Slater's gaze with his pale blue eyes. "It's nice to see you again."

Slater glanced around the office as he sat across the desk from him. There was only office furniture and a small table and chairs, on the wall above them a bland print of a vase full of hydrangeas, the blue kind, from somewhere else, not the pink ones you usually see in Southern California. But there was nothing personal, except maybe the other framed image, incongruous with the flower print—a photo of a mini jet airplane hanging on the wall behind his desk.

"We want to cooperate fully, and help in any way we can," Goff said.

"That's a very good attitude," Slater said.

"I can't remember exactly what your role is at Cudahy Mutual."

"I'm an investigator."

"I see. Our attorney provided a statement on behalf of the company, and you've seen Jason's statement, so I'm not sure what I can add."

"You could tell me why Jason is afraid of you."

Concern flashed in Goff's eyes. "Did he tell you that?"

"He wouldn't tell me anything."

Goff gestured helplessly. "He has no reason to be afraid of me. And what does that have to do with his insurance claim?"

Slater watched him for a moment. "Are you a pilot, Mr. Goff?"

"Why would you ask me that?"

"Well, besides the hotel-room hydrangeas, the only thing on the wall in your office is a photo of an airplane."

He laughed and leaned back in his chair, relieved. "Indeed. Yes, that's my baby."

"Yours, or the company's? It looks expensive."

"It's mine," Goff said, studying him. "I use it to get out of town on the weekend."

"Nice to have those kinds of resources. So why is there such tight security on this building? I thought you imported electronics."

"We do, but this is a rough neighborhood."

"No, it's not. I know people who live around here. This is working-class suburbia."

Goff shot him a thin smile. "Perhaps your perceptions are a little different."

Such a slimy desk jockey. So superior, in his own mind, because of the cut of his suit, or the color of his skin, or because he didn't have to fly commercial. No matter how special Goff thought he was, Slater had run across legions of these guys. He wanted to punch that grin off his face even more than before. Still, the pricey haircut, and the blond highlights—maybe they had something in common.

Slater stood, and Goff rose with him.

"You're kind of buff," Slater said, even though he couldn't really tell what his body was like under his suit. "Do you work out?"

Goff looked surprised. "Not lately."

"Maybe we can step out sometime, and you could show me what you've got." He pointedly looked down at Goff's pants. "I might be able to show you a thing or two. You know, make you happy." He dropped his chin and massaged the side pocket of his jeans—it seemed less lewd than actually grabbing his crotch—and held Goff's eyes. "Very happy."

"Mr. Ibáñez," Goff insisted, flustered now. "I'm a married man."

"To a woman, right? Kids?"

"Two."

"So when's the last time your wife went down on you?"

"That's none of your business," he snapped.

"I thought so. Lock the door, and I'll smoke you right now."

"Absolutely not," he said, his voice rising. "I don't swing that way."

Slater sighed. "Chump."

"Excuse me?" he demanded.

"Can you show me where the alleged accident

happened?"

Goff stared at him for a moment, blinking, but then moved around his desk, relieved to be escaping from the intensity of Slater's leer. He led the way down the stairs to the lobby, and pushed through the double doors just beyond Karen Chen's desk. She didn't even look up at them as they walked through.

They stepped into a huge industrial room, two stories high with a bare concrete floor and a pair of loading docks in the opposite wall, their doors rolled up and light flooding in. Two guys were packing shipping cartons with smaller corrugated boxes on a long work table. One of them looked up as they entered, but they kept working. Another table was piled with the small boxes and three trays of black plastic pieces. They looked like snap-together toy blocks, but from the way they were carefully arrayed and isolated from one another, these had to be valuable.

"What is all this crap?" Slater asked, watching the workers.

"It's not crap. We manufacture controllers for computerized systems," Goff said.

"You mean the Chinese manufacture them, and you import them, correct?"

Goff smiled. "The business is a little more complex than that, but yes, ultimately everything originates in China."

"What's a controller?"

"How well do you understand computers, Mr. Ibáñez, and robotics?"

"Not at all," Slater said, eyeing him. He was impressed that Goff had remembered his name, saying it more than once now and pronouncing it pretty well, using English vowels but getting the ñ right.

"Well, it's a little gizmo that tells other gizmos what to do."

Slater scoffed. "Sounds like my ex."

He wandered over to one side of the vast space, where industrial shelving went up many layers, to look at the blue-painted ladder fronting it.

"This is where Jason fell?" he asked.

"Allegedly," Goff said, trailing behind him.

It looked safe enough, more like stairs than a ladder, with a handrail on both sides. It was attached to a track running along the top, and Slater pushed the whole structure sideways a few feet, easily moving it on its path. He climbed on the bottom step, and felt the ladder sink slightly as his weight lowered it to the floor—a gravity brake that prevented it from moving while someone was on it. Grabbing the handrails and heaving his weight back and forth, it wouldn't budge.

"You see how difficult it would be to fall, if you were being attentive," Goff said, folding his arms and watching Slater step down. "My personal opinion is that this claim is a shakedown."

"Lucky for you, the insurance company is on the hook, not you."

Goff gestured vaguely. "Still, it will impact our premiums and our access to credit."

Slater looked around the room, at the loading bays open to the yard. There wasn't a truck in sight. Across the room from them, on the same wall as the door to the lobby, was another wide wooden door, this one with a number-pad lock on the handle.

"Where does that go?" Slater asked, gesturing to it.

"To the upper floors," Goff said quickly. "They're not in use."

His tone was firm, dismissive, and Slater searched his face. It felt like there was more to it, something Goff didn't want to talk about.

"Your office is upstairs, and it's in use."

"There are offices on that side of the building, but the old warehouse section is completely separate."

Slater walked casually toward the door, wondering if Goff would react. On the floor near the door jamb he noticed three little tan-colored balls. Those didn't look electronic. As he approached he dug his keys and a little stack of his business cards out of his pocket and fumbled with them, intentionally dropping them to the concrete floor, where the keys landed with a metallic *clink*. Making a show of crouching to pick them up, he scooped up two of the little objects and pocketed them with his keys, then turned back to Goff.

"I wanted to give you my contact information," he said, pulling a card from the stack and sliding the others into his pants pocket. "You can call me any time."

"Thank you," Goff said perfunctorily, glancing at it and slipping it into his breast pocket. Clearly he hadn't noticed Slater's subterfuge.

"When you get bored with waiting for women, I mean," Slater said.

Goff scowled. "I'm not anticipating that."

"Do you know what the difference is between parsley and pussy, Preston?"

"What?" Goff said, his tone rising, more a shocked reaction than a response to Slater's question.

Slater answered anyway. "Nothing—it's a waste of your time to eat either one."

Leaving Goff standing there, he walked back into the reception area and out to the street, grinning to himself. He glanced over his shoulder as he walked up the street toward his car, and satisfied that he wasn't being observed, fished the round little objects out of his jeans and looked at them. They were garbanzo beans, unmistakably—hard and uncooked. Why would an electronics company be keeping dry beans behind a locked door? Climbing into the Thunderbird, he examined them more closely in his palm. They were just garbanzo beans, nothing more. He dropped them in the ashtray and pulled out his tablet.

The Web knew more about Gislitech, and he dug through the sparse information on its website, which included professional portraits of Goff and the founder, Gil Martinson. He looked older than Goff, but it was difficult to tell from one image. Moving on to other sources, he read that Martinson was an entrepreneur who lived in Rolling Hills, way down on the Palos Verdes Peninsula, at least a half-hour's commute from here. It was hard to believe that Gislitech had only eight employees, and Slater double-checked with the website of the state tax regulator before he was convinced that was an accurate figure. The government categorized the company as an importer and manufacturer, even though all Slater had seen there were little black components being boxed up for shipping, and there weren't a lot of them. Maybe they had another facility somewhere else. But with eight employees, he'd already met half the workforce.

Stuffing his tablet into his satchel, he started the Thunderbird and pulled out, heading back toward the city. Jason was right—something shady was going on at Gislitech. The Web was a miasma of publicly available data, but he needed another kind of information, with more detail, from deeper down. Maybe there was a reason he'd run into Conrad last night. If he was going to ask for his help, though, Slater was going to have to swallow his pride, and check his anger.

Being a cop, Conrad was tuned in to human nature, but he had trusted Slater enough to let him see the four-digit code he used to get into his phone. Slater grinned at the memory. What a dumbass. Back when things were rough between them but they were still together, that had allowed him to install a hidden tracking app on Conrad's phone. It wasn't about stalking, Slater reminded himself, but rather a useful tool he had access to as an investigator. He'd do it to any of his targets if he had the opportunity.

Conrad would do the same thing to the perps he needed to follow, if he could, but as a cop his tactics were far more limited. Meeting with a sleazy Russian tech vendor on a grimy backstreet in Glendale to buy surveillance gear was just business for Slater, but if Conrad showed up in a place like that, everyone would assume it was a bust.

Traffic on the freeway had slowed to a crawl, and Slater set his phone in his lap, pulling up the tracking app and glancing at it briefly when he had to come to a stop. Conrad's phone was at Rampart, the police station in Slater's neighborhood, which meant Conrad was there too.

Perfect, he thought, and headed there, moving slowly in the afternoon congestion on the freeway and on the surface streets. Parking in front of the station, he checked the tracking app again to confirm Conrad was still here, and then phoned him.

"What do you need, Slater? I'm working," he said when he picked up.

"Are you on patrol today, or at your office?" Slater asked. "Come and talk to me. I'm out front."

"Why are you here?" Conrad demanded.

"I just need two minutes of your time."

Conrad sighed audibly and ended the call. A minute later he emerged from the building's entrance, glaring at Slater, who was walking up the steps from the street. It must be an office day, Slater thought, as he was in uniform but wasn't wearing his vest or his weapon. Conrad beckoned him away from the doorway, where they might be overheard, and walked a few steps down the accessibility ramp, pausing next to a globe mallow bush. The city must have decided to replace the lawn with drought-tolerant landscaping, and it did look a lot more interesting than grass, its chains of rusty orange flowers in full bloom.

"How's the hangover?" Conrad asked, folding his arms.

Slater took a breath. "Normally I'd say fuck you, Conrad, but I need you to do something."

He frowned. "What?"

"I'm working a case, and I need more info on a company and a couple of its principle players. Something fishy is going on, and I want to see what spews out of your police computers."

"No way. I could get in a lot of trouble."

"Not if you're careful about it. I know you're a smart guy."

"Even so," Conrad said, "Why would I do that for you?"

"Well, there's an incentive. I still have some juicy photos of you with my dick in your mouth. I could email them to your sergeant, or your watch commander, or whoever your boss is."

Slater had anticipated an angry reaction, but Conrad just laughed.

"That's the second time in two days you've talked about me blowing you. Does that give you a feeling of power or something?"

Slater looked down. "No. I guess I kind of miss it."

"You know that if you sent out photos like that, I'd be embarrassed for a shift or two, until everyone had heard the story and seen the pictures and teased me about it. Ultimately, though, nobody in there cares who I sleep with. You, however, would be charged with distributing revenge porn."

"I'm willing to take that risk," Slater said. "Are

you willing to take on the embarrassment?"

Conrad shook his head. "You're like a sad song, Slater. The kind that makes me sad, even if I don't want to hear it."

"And you're my kryptonite," Slater said quietly. "You make me act like an asshole."

"I'm glad that you know you do that."

Conrad put his hands on his hips and looked him in the eye. He was just the same height as Slater, which had made the sex so much better, Slater remembered, with no need to compensate for it, always in the perfect position. He pushed that memory away.

"I'll do this for you," Conrad said, "but not because of your lame threat to blackmail me. That's super trashy, by the way, besides being illegal, in case you didn't know. I'll do this for you because I respect you."

"That sounds far-fetched," Slater said, "but thank you. I'll email you the names."

"I can probably get you something by the end of shift tonight." Conrad's face broke into a grin. "Do you really have photos like that? I don't remember you taking any."

Of course he didn't—he would never do that. But he said, "Let's hope you never have to find out."

Turning to walk to his car, Slater had to force himself not to look back.

THREE

KOREATOWN WAS PRACTICALLY on the way home, just a few blocks' drive, and Slater stopped at a diner he knew in a strip mall, parking out front. As soon as he sat at the counter a waiter stepped over, a thin guy, with visible but non-gym pecs, wearing a funny paper hat that was pointed at the back and front like an old military cap. Slater ordered *bibimbap* without looking at the menu.

"Want me to throw some beef on top?" the waiter asked.

"Just the vegetables, thanks. Skip the egg too."

Little bowls of side dishes appeared one by one while he waited for the hot dish, and tucking into one, shoveling with his chopsticks, he realized he really was hungry.

The waiter set down the *bibimbap*. "You eat like a Korean," he said.

Slater glanced up at him and pulled the bowl closer. "Is that a good thing or a bad thing?"

"My mother thinks it's a good thing." He nodded to the other end of the counter.

Slater glanced over to see a woman standing at the cash register, not looking at them but running a transaction for someone.

"You don't like the fish?" the waiter said, collecting the empty side bowls.

"I didn't even try it," Slater said, stirring veggies and tofu into the rice. "I'm vegan."

"That's surprising, from a guy who looks like you."

Slater looked up at him, eyes narrowing. "That sounds a little judgmental. Didn't your mother ever tell you not to judge a book by its cover?"

"Probably. She also told me to watch out for guys who wear tight jeans in ninety-degree heat."

Slater chuckled. "I guess I should have checked the weather when I got up."

"Don't get me wrong. They look fine," he said. "Real fine."

Slater sat up straighter. "Are you hitting on me?" It wasn't something that happened very often, especially with twinks.

"That depends," the waiter said. "Do you think

you can handle it?"

"You're a cocky bastard," Slater said, grinning at him. "How old are you?"

"Old enough to know what I want."

Probably around thirty, Slater thought, looking him over, and decided to point it out. "What's your name, son?"

"It's Keith. I get off in a couple of hours, if you're going to be around."

Slater nodded. "Why don't you call me then? Have you got a pencil?"

Keith pulled out his phone and thumb-typed as Slater recited his number.

"Now, would you let me finish my dinner?" Slater said.

Keith grinned and walked away.

After he'd eaten he got up and paid Keith's mother at the register, wondering if she knew her son was arranging hookups while he was working. The drive home was quick, despite the traffic, as Slater knew which side streets moved faster.

Once he was upstairs he picked up the clothes strewn around his bed and threw them in the bottom of the closet for Rosa, then unpacked the bourbon bottles he'd bought last night and put them in a kitchen cupboard. From the one that was already open, he poured himself a single shot and dropped in an ice cube, then put the bottle out of sight in a cupboard. He didn't want to get soused before his date called, if he really was going to call.

Taking that first sip and savoring the flavor, he set the glass on the floor beside the sofa, then turned on the stereo and stretched out, digging around on his phone to find a sasquatch podcast, sinking into the cushions with his arm over his eyes as it started. He got lost in the host's hypnotic narration of the squatchers' excursions into the deep woods, where they encountered mysterious fibers caught on tree branches, massive footprints in the mud of a riverbank, an eerie call in the moonlit forest.

Slater wasn't really sure how he felt about the sasquatch, or what it meant, but the audio carried him out of his everyday grind, away from fraud and spying on deadbeats, away from this crappy apartment. With *Sasquatch Search* there was only the forest, the mystery, the quest for the cryptic beast.

———·———

WAKING, HE WAS DISORIENTED. It was dark outside. His phone was ringing—that's what had woken him. He reached down and scrabbled for it on the carpet. It was an unfamiliar number in the 213 area code—that was downtown, and Koreatown. It was the waiter.

"Ibáñez," he answered.

"It's Keith, from the diner."

"I remember," Slater said. "I live near there. You can come over here, or I can come to you."

"It's better if I come there. I still live with my mom."

"OK. Do you like camping?"

"Sure, I guess," Keith said. "Why?"

"Because my place is a little like that. There's no food, I sleep on a futon, and the bathroom makes my cleaning woman blush."

"I'm sure I can handle it," he said, and Slater rattled off his address.

Just a few minutes later, he knocked on the door, and Slater pulled it open for him. Keith was wearing a white T-shirt now, accentuating the pleasing shape of his torso.

"You weren't kidding," he said, stepping in and looking around. "This is a depression apartment."

"What does that mean?" Slater asked dubiously, closing the door and twisting the deadbolt.

"It's dark, and it needs paint, and I can't tell if your carpet has a pattern in it or if it's just stains. This is the kind of apartment you'd rent if you were depressed."

"Blow me," Slater said.

Keith laughed, stepping into the living room.

"I'm serious," Slater said, walking around the island and pulling open his belt buckle. "Get on your knees."

Keith held up a finger. "I will do that, but first, let me explain. I don't want to be bossed around and roughed up."

Slater paused, his belt buckle hanging free, and put his hands on his hips. "I guess I'm the one making assumptions now."

"I'm sure you get that a lot," Keith said. "I mean, you're kind of built for it. I hope it's OK that I don't want that."

"I rough people up for a living," Slater said. "I don't need to do it when I'm fucking them."

"OK, good," Keith said, and nodded.

"So what is it that you do want?"

"I'm more interested in the paternal type. Not the angry disciplinarian, but the nurturing supportive dad."

Slater laughed. "A man who knows what he wants. I can definitely work with that."

"Do you party?" Keith asked. "I have some rock, and some weed."

"Would you do those with your father?"

"Probably not."

"So there's you're answer."

Keith frowned. "Weed is legal now, you know."

"So is Pilates," Slater said flatly, "but I'm not doing that either. Nobody's doing drugs in my house."

"Fine," he said, and threw up his hands.

Slater dropped to one knee, his knuckles on

the carpet, and said, "Piggyback."

Keith didn't budge. "What?"

"Move it, son," he insisted. "Climb on board."

"Oh." He moved behind Slater and wrapped his arms around his shoulders, his knees around his waist.

Slater stood up, wobbling with the extra weight but keeping his balance, and spun around, making Keith grasp more tightly and crack up laughing.

"Duck," Slater said, and walked through the bedroom doorway, stooping so they'd both fit, and then tumbling with him onto the bed.

Rolling onto his back, Keith was laughing, exhilarated, his eyes bright. His hard cock was visible in his pants, and Slater gently massaged it, and kissed him, and took his time undressing him. Pulling off his own clothes, he explored Keith's body, moving slowly, sensuously, holding him tight for a moment and then moving on with his hands.

He gradually worked his fingers inside him, and Keith arched his back, easing into it, still rock-hard. When Slater entered him, he barely reacted, catching his breath and closing his eyes. Slater moved slowly, carefully, increasing the rhythm and building intensity. Keith came quickly, his body throbbing, and Slater stopped to let it happen, his hands firm on his waist.

What is it about being young that made sex so easy, so fast? As he got older, his desire wasn't waning at all, but his performance was gradually slowing. Wrapping his arms around Keith's sweaty torso, now calm and relaxed, he resumed the rhythm, thrusting into him, relishing the heat of his body, inhaling the scent of his hair until he came.

After he'd caught his breath, he pulled out and peeled off the condom, tossing it toward the bathroom. Keith was already talking.

"You called me a bastard," he was saying, "which is kind of ironic, because I am a bastard. I guess that's why I'm into the whole dad thing. My mother was a single parent. She came here on her own from Korea."

"North Korea, or South Korea?" Slater asked. Of course she was South Korean, he knew that, but he also knew that question was a great way to wind people up.

"Are you freaking kidding me?" Keith said, his voice rising. "Do you know how hard it is to get out of North Korea? People are starving ..."

Lying on his back and grinning to himself, Slater tuned him out, and put his arm over his eyes. His mind went back to Gislitech, the odd vibe of that building, Goff's sanitized office, the sense he got that something was just off. Was there a connection between Jason's injury and the company? Was the company in on the insurance scam? It was hard to see how they would benefit, and even if Jason was kicking part of the payout back to them, it wasn't all that much money, at least not at the corporate scale. Maybe it was just Goff.

Finally there was a break in the talking.

"You can stay, if you want," Slater said.

"Cool," Keith said, and sat up. "I'll just text my mom."

"Do you want a drink?"

Keith shook his head, already typing on his phone.

In the kitchen Slater opened the cupboard and pulled out the open bottle of bourbon, raising it to his lips and guzzling, squeezing his eyes shut to enjoy the sweet burn. He was under no delusion that this was to be savored—right now he needed it to knock him out.

He'd only taken an initial pull from the bottle, the first of the several he'd planned, when he heard his phone buzz, and went back to the bedroom to check. It was a text from Conrad, and he leaned on the door frame to read it, the painted wood cool against his bare back.

Got some dirt on your tech company. Call me.

Slater texted back:

Can you just send me a printout?

His reply came a few seconds later:

No way. From my eyes to your ears—no email
trail.

Slater sighed and turned to walk into the living room.

"Where are you going?" Keith asked.

"I have to make a call. I'll be back."

Fishing his tablet out of his satchel, he dropped onto the sofa and dialed Conrad.

"Good timing," Conrad said. "I just got home."

"So what did you find?"

"Gislitech got audited four years ago. The taxman thought there was way too much revenue for the number of people working there."

"I wondered about that," Slater said, making notes on his tablet, cradling the phone to his ear with his shoulder. "They only have eight employees."

"The feds never cited them or charged them, which means they didn't find anything."

"Their only business is electronic hardware, correct? Did you run across any mention of food? Garbanzo beans?"

"Nothing like that," Conrad said. "They only deal in one kind of thing. It's called a controller."

"What about the staff?"

"Your friend Goff at Gislitech is pretty clean. He got sued in a stock fraud case when he worked as a financial adviser, and if I'm reading it right, he's not allowed to do that work anymore, even though the case was settled before trial. Since then he's kept his nose clean. He's got a wife, two kids."

"Yeah, I heard about the happy family when I interviewed him."

"Why would he share that with you? It seems kind of personal."

"Straight guys do that, asserting their heterosexuality," Slater said. "They assume because you're a gay guy, you're automatically interested in them."

"I don't think I ever noticed that," Conrad said dubiously.

"If you were anywhere nearly as good-looking as me, it would happen all the time."

Conrad laughed heartily, too long and too loud, Slater thought. A bit of a buzz from the bourbon was encroaching on his thoughts, but he shook it off.

"What about Martinson?" Slater asked.

"He's more interesting. There's no record of him before he immigrated, about fifteen years ago."

"From where?"

"His passport is Icelandic. His original name

is Gísli. That's why the company has that weird name. When he bought his green card to stay here, he chose to go by Gil. No spouse or any record of a spouse, but he emigrated with a daughter. Her name is Agnes."

"OK," Slater said, scribbling notes on his tablet.

"A few months ago he was detained at Calexico for three days. They thought he was up to something, probably because he crossed in and out six times in less than a month."

"Smuggling?"

"The report doesn't say that, but I assume that's what they suspected. He was released without charge, so they didn't catch him with anything."

"How could they hold him for three days without charging him?"

"Noncitizen, at the border, not yet in the country—he had no constitutional rights. Border control can do whatever they want. There was a note in the file that I didn't understand, though. One of the investigators wrote 'the Indians,' with a question mark."

"The Indians," Slater said, making note of it. "What does that mean?"

"No idea, and I know what you're going to say"—Conrad lowered his voice and slurred his words—"'Just call her, dumbass, and ask her what it means.' But I can't do that. I'm not supposed to be looking, and if I ask, it'll be, 'Why are you asking?' People get shit-canned all the time for looking at stuff they're not supposed to. And this is Homeland Security—those people don't mess around."

"I get it," Slater said. "You can't pursue it." He finished his notes and set down the tablet, rubbing his eyes. "I guess I should thank you for doing this."

"I'm saving you from yourself, Slater. This way, your dick pics won't be all over the Internet, and I won't have to write you up for revenge porn."

"I'd never try to get revenge on you, buddy. You're too good to me."

It sounded sappy, and weak, he knew, his guard lowered by the booze. He regretted saying it when he knew Conrad had picked up on it.

"Yeah? Well, don't you forget it," he said gruffly, and ended the call.

The bottle of bourbon was still on the kitchen counter, and he took a few good pulls before heading into the bedroom. It was dark—Keith had turned out the light—and Slater climbed onto the futon to find him still and quiet, thankfully. Settling in, he turned on his side, and as he was sinking into sleep, Keith wrapped his arms around his chest and folded his knee into the back of Slater's. Despite the sweaty heat, it felt good.

FOUR

O PENING HIS EYES, still half asleep, he started awake when he saw Keith's face a few inches away, staring at him.

"How did you get this?" Keith asked, reaching out and tracing a line on the side of his chin.

"In a fight," Slater said, blinking and trying to remember this guy's name.

"It looks like it must have hurt. So did you know that you snore?"

"I don't snore," Slater said firmly.

"You sort of do. Maybe it's the booze. When you came to bed, you smelled like the hard stuff."

Slater sat up. "I have to go to work. Can I drop you somewhere?"

"I left my car outside on your street."

"Really? I hope it's still there."

"I was wondering about that—why do you live in such a shitty neighborhood?"

"What are you, a cub reporter now?" Slater said, irritated, and got up. Turning back, he asked, more gently, "Do you want a coffee?"

"Sure," Keith said, cheerful and unfazed, and started to climb off the futon.

Slater went to pee and then into the kitchen, where he filled two mugs with tap water and set them in the microwave, then went back to the bedroom to get dressed. It was probably stupid to wear a black shirt in the blazing sun and summer heat, but that's what was clean, so he pulled on his jeans and tucked it in.

He spooned powdered instant coffee into the steaming mugs and stirred them, leaving one on the counter for Keith, who soon came out of the bathroom, wearing the red plaid boxer shorts Slater had pulled off him last night.

"This tastes like bong water," Keith said, sipping at the mug and wrinkling his nose.

"You're welcome," Slater said.

"You people are usually way more granola."

"What are you talking about?" Slater demanded, gulping at his mug.

"You're the least granola vegan I've ever met. Why are you even vegan?"

"I know lots of people who need to be slapped around and locked up. That doesn't extend to animals."

Slater put his mug in the sink and went to look in the bathroom mirror. He needed a shave, but he couldn't bring himself to be bothered, and splashed water on his face. Back in the kitchen his phone went off—a personalized ring that made his heart sink. *"No wire hangers,"* the woman's voice shrieked through the tinny little speaker. *"I buy you beautiful dresses, and you treat them like they were some dishrag ..."*

He dried his hands and went back to retrieve his phone from the counter.

"Super annoying ring tone," Keith said.

Slater ignored him and picked up. "Yes, Mother—what do you need?" he said impatiently.

"Lunch," she said. "I thought it was time you met Albert."

"Who?" he demanded.

"Albert," she said, louder, as if he hadn't heard. "We've been seeing each other for a while."

"I don't need to meet your boyfriend," Slater said.

"I think you'll like him. I'm going to make a chopped salad with that phony mayonnaise you like."

"I don't have time to drop everything and rearrange my day to suit you, Doris."

"So kick him out of bed and send him home,"

she said. "I'm sure you can manage that by lunch-time."

Slater glanced at Keith, leaning against the counter, absorbed in the screen on his phone.

"I'm working," he snapped.

"Everyone has time for lunch. It'll just take an hour of your day. Bring a bottle of red. Albert likes that Two-Buck Chuck."

"Fine," he said, through gritted teeth, and ended the call.

"You are really hard on her," Keith said, looking up from his phone.

"She doesn't even notice," he said, and squeezed his eyes shut to think. It was the last thing he wanted to do today, but he could make time for it, of course, and he could easily limit it to an hour.

"You only get one mother," Keith said.

Slater focused on him, furrowing his brow, and raised his voice. "I don't need advice from you."

"Of course not," Keith said, glancing up, not noticing or not concerned about the edge in Slater's tone. "I'm just saying."

Slater scoffed and started unbuttoning his shirt, hanging it on the back of the bathroom door. Leaning into the mirror, he set to work shaving off his whiskers. If he was going to see Doris today, it was something he had to do.

Once his shirt was on again, he went back into the kitchen. "I have to go," he said, grabbing his satchel.

"I'm not even dressed yet," Keith protested. "Can I let myself out?"

Pulling open a kitchen drawer, Slater found the spare key, and handed it to him. "Lock the deadbolt, then slide the key under the door."

Keith took it and grinned at him. "What if I hang on to it?"

"Then I'd hunt you down, and kick your ass."

"I believe you would," he said, his levity fading.

Slater kissed him good-bye and left, trotting down the stairs. He didn't usually let people hang out in his place, but there was nothing much to steal, and Keith knew that Slater knew where his mother worked, even what she looked like. He wouldn't be there for long anyway—it really wasn't a comfortable place to linger.

———•———

ON THE FREEWAY HE headed east, back to Gislitech. He wasn't in a rush, but he drove hard, as he always did, not weaving around like a hooligan but changing lanes when he could get a speed advantage. The car was built for it.

Thinking about what Conrad had told him, he mulled over *Indians,* the word, the idea. It

57

could be the old name for Native Americans, or a racist sports team. More likely, though, since it was something a border control investigator had written down, it meant people from India.

Those birds of paradise were ripe and ready to pop open, any day now, given this heat, he thought, walking past them into the lobby of the Gislitech building. Karen Chen was on the reception desk again, and as he approached, Slater greeted her, "Hey, beautiful."

She smiled sweetly and said, "Hey, Neanderthal."

"Ouch," he said, leaning on the counter. "Why am I a Neanderthal for thinking that you're beautiful?" He doubted it was something she heard very often, what with that busted nose.

"Because I don't want to be treated like a piece of meat."

"See, I do, so that makes no sense to me at all."

"Would you say the same thing to a man?"

Slater nodded. "Oh, yeah—even if he wasn't beautiful."

She scowled at him. "Is there something you need, Mr. Ibáñez?"

He grinned at her. "You remembered my name."

"Brother, I've got your number."

"I need to talk to Goff again. Just for a minute."

She sighed and picked up the phone. "Mr. Ibáñez to see you." She listened, and glanced up at Slater. "I think he already knows you're in."

"I'll just go up, then," Slater said, even though she was still on the phone, and went to the stairs, bounding up them two at a time, ignoring her call to "Wait."

Goff was in his office, with the door open, talking into the handset of his desk phone, wearing another new suit.

"Don't bother. I'll get rid of him myself," Goff said, and hung up.

"Don't look so stressed out, Preston. I just got here," Slater said, and dropped into a chair.

"Well?" he said, raising his eyebrows.

"So does your airplane have a name, like your kids presumably do, or do you just call it 'my airplane'?"

"Mr. Ibáñez," he said carefully, "What do you want?"

"I have a couple more questions. How is it that you do umpteen millions of dollars in business but only employ eight people? Your Uncle Sam wanted to know that too. How did you convince him you were legit?"

"We subcontract the manufacturing," Goff said, his tone guarded, but then he leaned back in his chair and laced his fingers behind his head. "Our products are of high value. Think of it like diamonds. They're cheap to dig out of the ground, but the markup is huge—thousands of times what it cost to obtain them."

"OK," Slater said, watching him. Diamonds were run by a cartel, and not many industries worked like that—certainly not one that hawked little bits of black plastic manufactured in China. But he didn't challenge Goff on it. The guy clearly assumed he was stupid, which might be useful. When people underestimated him, it made them overconfident, and much easier to outsmart.

"Where's Gil Martinson's office?" Slater said. "I should have a word with him."

"Gil doesn't come in very often. He works from home most days."

"In Rolling Hills, right?"

Goff frowned. "He's not available now. I can ask his assistant to call you, if it's absolutely necessary, but he's a busy man. Gil wasn't here the day the alleged accident happened."

"What's his assistant's name?" Slater asked. "For when he calls me."

"Max."

"One other thing," Slater said, leaning toward him. "I got to thinking. If I was in your shoes, being Jason's boss and all, it would be pretty easy to arrange a little slip-and-fall, send Jason for an MRI and home for bed rest, and then split the insurance payout with him. A few hundred grand would buy a lot of toilet paper for your airplane."

"That's extremely offensive," Goff snapped, sitting up.

"But you didn't say it's not true."

"I have no reason to do that. My salary and benefits far outweigh any insurance payment Jason might get. Gislitech is privately held, so the managers get a sizeable share of the profits."

"All two of you."

"Three, actually."

"We know there are big profits," Slater said, "so you're getting rich just by sitting there."

Goff shot him a thin smile. "I do work for what I earn."

"What can you tell me about the Indians?" Slater asked, watching him closely.

A flash of fear flitted through Goff's eyes, and he cleared his throat, looking down at his desktop, picking up a sheet of paper and moving it to the side. "I have no idea what you're talking about."

"Are you sure about that?"

Goff recovered his composure. "Mr. Ibáñez, I've got things to do, and I don't see anything more I can help you with. You need to leave. You won't be welcome here again."

Finally, Slater thought, he was showing some backbone. He rose and planted his palms on Goff's desk, jutting his jaw toward him. Goff recoiled involuntarily, sinking back in his chair.

"If you refuse to talk to me," Slater said intently, "or interfere with my investigation in any other way, I'll have Cudahy Mutual void your insurance, and I'll tell them you're personally complicit in trying to defraud them."

He held Goff's eyes, full of that familiar surprise and anger and fear.

"I'm sure the last thing Gil wants is to be left uninsured," Slater continued. "In the industry, the technical term for that is 'tits up on the pavement.'"

"Get out," Goff snapped.

Slater straightened up and shifted to a casual tone. "Anyway, I know you've got things to do. Those controllers aren't going to ship themselves, right? Call me if you ever want to talk, Preston, or if you get tired of not having sex."

As Slater walked toward the door, Goff called after him.

"You need professional help," he said sharply.

"You mean a shrink?" Slater said, turning back. "Shrinks are fun. I've bonked a few. Usually I wind up helping them more than they help me."

Walking out of the office and down the stairs, he had to grin. It was all bluster—he had no power to alter anyone's insurance coverage. Della would laugh in his face if he even suggested such a thing. But he'd touched a nerve by mentioning the Indians. There was definitely something there.

Back in his car, he cranked up the air-conditioning and headed for the freeway. Extracting a glimmer of information from Goff was a cakewalk compared with the grim task ahead—lunch with Doris.

Years ago, when she was still teaching, but after Slater had escaped her orbit, she'd bought a little bungalow in Mount Washington, when it had been a shitty neighborhood and real estate was still cheap. Slater wished she'd sell it, now that it was gentrified, and cash in, move up the coast like a normal retiree, but she seemed intent on staying in town. Too close, he thought, merging onto the Arroyo Parkway. Even in a city of ten million people, she was too close.

He made a quick detour to a liquor store just off the freeway, picking out the cheapest rotgut red he could find that was actually in a glass bottle. Fuck Albert and his Two-Buck Chuck. It wasn't pretentious, he had to admit, because it really did cost two dollars, or close to it, and the cheapest bottle he could find here was eight. But he wasn't going any farther out of his way to buy that. Albert could drink this or do without.

Doris's familiar Buick was in the driveway, and beside it sat a red Porsche Boxster with the top down, parked at a stupid angle, as if it were insisting on being noticed, like a drunken twinkie at Pride wearing flip-flops and a thong. It had to be Albert's car, and it made him hate the guy before they'd even met.

Slater pulled the Thunderbird up tight to the Boxster's ugly rear end and set the parking brake. His trunk was blocking the sidewalk, he knew, but it was a quiet hillside street, so it was unlikely he'd get cited. Even if he did, it would be worth it to make a point: Albert was in his way.

Grabbing the paper bag with the bottle in it, he climbed out and went to the front door, calling out "I'm here" as he walked in, not bothering to knock.

Doris stepped out of the dining room and embraced him, craning up to kiss his freshly smooth cheek. She'd always been slight, and kept her dark hair short, these days letting a little gray show in it. Today, despite the heat, she was wearing a black turtleneck, a silver ring on a long necklace hanging on top.

"You look tired," she said, stepping back to look him over. "Have you been sleeping?"

Ignoring the question, he asked, "Did you invite one of your girlfriends?"

She frowned. "Why would you say that? It's just you and me and Albert."

"There's a woman's car in your driveway," Slater said.

"The Porsche?" Albert said, stepping out of the kitchen, grinning at him and wiping his hands on a towel. "That's mine."

"The infamous Albert," Slater said, pointedly looking him up and down and handing him the paper bag with the bottle. He was short, and dumpy, and wore a comb-over and a stupid Hawaiian shirt. Doris could do so much better.

Albert introduced himself, cradling the paper bag and its contents in both hands, like it was something fragile and invaluable.

Doris grabbed Slater's upper arm, giving it a firm squeeze. "My son," she said emphatically. "Isn't he adorable? I'm so glad you two finally get to meet."

She shepherded Slater into the dining room, where places were set on the table. Doris and Albert went into the kitchen and returned with the food, chopped salad, as promised, along with something that looked like another salad, as well as bread and some olives. Slater waited until they sat, then took the chair opposite Albert, and folded his arms.

"Why are you driving a German car?" Slater asked him. "Are you Jewish?"

"I'm not," Albert said, his eyebrows rising, flicking his napkin into his lap.

Slater looked at Doris. "He's not even Jewish."

Doris laughed. "Neither was your father."

"I didn't know it was a requirement," Albert said.

"It's not, sweetie," Doris said, patting his hand.

Slater scoffed and averted his gaze.

"It was too hot to cook, so everything's cold," she said, pointing at each of the dishes in turn. "I used fake mayo in this one, this is fake cream cheese, and the baguette is completely dairy-free."

"Just because it doesn't have animal products in it doesn't mean it's fake," Slater said irritably, and helped himself to the chopped salad.

The wine hadn't appeared, he noticed. Perhaps buying it had just been an errand for Albert, and they weren't going to share it. More likely, though, it hadn't passed muster.

"So, Slater, what do you do for a living?" Albert asked, scooping from one of the bowls onto his plate.

"She didn't tell you?" he said, eyeing him. "I'm in insurance."

"A claims investigator," Doris said. "They keep him busy too. No time for romance."

"You don't know anything about that part of my life," Slater said. "I do just fine."

"I'm not talking about your sex life," she said, gesturing with her fork. "I'm talking about meeting a nice guy and settling down, getting married."

"So you're gay," Albert said, raising his eyebrows.

"Yeah—you want to fight about it?" Slater asked, glaring at him.

Albert winced. "No," he said quickly. "I mean, good for you."

"Settle down," Doris said, tapping Slater on the forearm. "There's no need to be hostile." Turning to Albert, she said, "Forgive Slater's manners. I like to call him my diamond in the rough."

"I can understand why he's protective," Albert said, focusing on his plate. "You're his mother."

"In middle school they thought he could channel all that aggression into wrestling," Doris said, swiping cheese onto a chunk of baguette. "That lasted for a while, and then in high school the solution was physical labor. They got him into a horticulture program. Slater put in all those roses in the backyard, and the Southwestern landscaping."

"It's a beautiful yard," Albert said.

"Mother, please," Slater demanded, feeling his face heating up. "I don't do that anymore."

"He's found his niche now, though," Doris said, reaching up and ruffling Slater's hair.

"So what do you do, Albert?" Slater asked. "Did you buy that toy car outright, or is it a lease?"

"I'm an orthopedic surgeon," he said, popping an olive into his mouth and talking around it. "I fix knees."

"That sounds extremely boring."

Albert laughed. "It is, I suppose. But it's extremely profitable. And the car is just for fun.

Like a hobby."

"Slater's quite interested in the sasquatch," Doris said. "That's almost like his hobby."

"Oh, my god, Mother—shut up," Slater said.

"Seriously?" Albert said, grinning like an idiot now. "Do you go tracking them in the woods?"

"No," Slater snapped. "It's not like that."

"Well, it's important to have other interests," Albert said, shrugging. "All work and no play, as they say."

Slater rolled his eyes and fumed, pushing cubes of broccoli and carrot around in the mayonnaise on his plate. It was none of anybody's business, and it made him want to punch the smarmy smirk off Albert's face. But he bit his tongue, for Doris's sake—he had to try, at least, to be civil. Shifting in his chair, he pushed aside the frustration and worked to engage with them, answering their questions, listening to Albert talk about his life, and the two of them laughing as they recounted driving up to San Luis Obispo in his doll car.

"Sounds like a nice place to retire," Slater said pointedly.

When they'd finished eating, Albert stacked their plates and set them at the side of the table.

"I found a vegan cheesecake," Doris said, clapping her hands. "How fun is that?" She rose and went into the kitchen.

"I'm so glad I met your mother," Albert said, once they were alone. "She's such a delight."

Slater knew what he was doing: filling up the space with words because the quiet made him uncomfortable.

"How well do you know her?" Slater asked, dubious. "I mean, how long have you been seeing each other?"

"A few months. It's going really well—she makes me happy."

"Let's hope things continue in that vein," Slater said. "Because if you make her cry, or harm even one hair on her head, I will rip your balls off and shove them down your throat."

Albert blinked rapidly, staring at him. "What?"

"You heard me," Slater said quietly, eyes narrowing. "Then I'll dump your unconscious body in that toy car of yours and push it off a cliff up on Mulholland."

Doris came back into the room, balancing three little plates with wedges of cheesecake on them.

"Yum," Slater said, grinning up at her. "I never get vegan cheesecake."

FIVE

S HE WAS leaving, Slater gave Doris a hug, then took her hands in his, looking her in the eye. "Remember our rule about guys?" he asked.

She grinned at him. "You don't have to worry. This one's the right kind."

"What's your rule about guys?" Albert asked, standing behind her, hands on his hips, that annoying grin on his face again.

Why did he have to ask? Slater wondered, shooting him a look. Why couldn't he just mind his own goddamn business?

"I'm only supposed to date guys who'll mess up my lipstick, not my mascara," Doris said, turning back to him. "It's an old girl-power expression."

"Smart," Albert said, and then asked Slater, "Do you have the same rule?"

"I don't wear mascara," Slater said flatly.

"Not since high school, anyway," Doris said, folding her arms.

Slater chuckled. "That was guyliner. Totally different."

Walking out to the street, he felt lighter, glad to be done with them, and scoffed one last time at Albert's stupid car before he backed the Thunderbird out and headed away from Doris's neighborhood. Besides Conrad, she was the only other person on the planet who could make him feel things that couldn't be fixed with a sharp right hook.

Back to work, he thought, pushing away those thoughts. He put his phone in his lap, and using the speaker, dialed Gabe, a guy who worked for him from time to time.

"*Hola,* Slater," Gabe answered.

"Hey, man—are you working today? I want to borrow your truck."

"I had a job this morning, but I'm finished. You'll have to gas it up."

"Excellent," Slater said, and navigated to Lincoln Heights, pulling the Thunderbird to the curb up the street from Gabe's driveway, where his familiar white truck was parked.

Gabe made his living as a painter, and his

truck was customized for that—locking cabinets lining the bed, ladders and brooms strapped in and cable-locked along the top.

At the side of the house Slater rapped on the heavy security door, an inner-city version of a screen door with bars to let the breeze through, immaculately painted white. A little girl, no older than five or six, and with Gabe's dark, wide-set eyes, came to look between the bars.

"Hi, sweetheart," Slater said, dropping to a crouch. "Is your father home?"

She nodded solemnly and turned to call inside, *"Papá."*

Gabe appeared, in jeans and a work shirt, looking harried and cradling an infant.

"Hold him for a second, yeah?" Gabe said, pushing open the door and handing over the wispy-haired baby, wearing a puffy diaper and a little T-shirt.

Slater took the kid, one hand under each of his tiny arms, and watched Gabe disappear. Babies needed neck support, he knew, but this one seemed to be old enough to hold his own head up. Slater bobbed him up and down, and the child watched him with interest.

"You're heavy," Slater told him. "What are they feeding you, rocks?"

There were voices inside, and Gabe's wife appeared, speaking to Slater in Spanish, which happened a lot, because Slater looked like he should understand. He couldn't remember her name—something with an *L*—but the tone of it was apologetic, so he grinned and just said *"Gracias,"* handing over the child.

As she went inside, the baby was still watching him over her shoulder.

"Stay in school, kid," he called to him.

Gabe returned and hustled him outside, closing the door. "Sorry—busy day. How long do you need the truck?"

"I'm thinking maybe I need you too, if you're available. Can I hire you both for a couple of hours? I need to go to the South Bay. Rolling Hills."

"That whole place is gated. You won't get in without an appointment."

"That's why I need your truck."

Gabe grinned. "We're going in stealth mode?"

"Right. Do you have a pair of coveralls for me?"

Unlocking one of the cabinets in the bed of his truck, Gabe pulled out a pair and handed them to Slater, then started pulling on his own. They were white but stained with dozens of drips and swipes of paint in a wide gamut of colors. It was too hot for this, Slater thought, but he knew the truck had air.

"You'll need your ID," Slater said, once they were both dressed.

Gabe went wordlessly back to the house,

knowing what he meant—the fake ID Slater had given him for jobs like this. Latino new arrivals did most of the manual labor in Los Angeles, and for that reason guys who looked like Slater and Gabe could fit in anywhere in town. They looked like they were supposed to be here, painting or gardening or doing some other grunt work that more established people refused to do, and Slater often used it to his advantage.

Once he'd returned, Gabe got in behind the wheel, and Slater climbed in the other side, cranking up the air. They hadn't even left the neighborhood when Gabe turned into a gas station and pulled up to a pump.

"Can you pay?" Gabe asked him.

"Of course." Slater climbed out and went to grab the nozzle.

"Use the high-octane," Gabe said, poking his head out the driver's window.

"You know that stuff is a rip-off, right?" Slater said. "This isn't a sports car."

"High-octane," Gabe insisted.

"You're the boss," Slater said, grinning at him and pushing the button for the more expensive grade before he started fueling.

Once they were on the freeway, Gabe took a call from his wife, patiently arguing with her about something in Spanish. Lupe, that was her name, Slater remembered, as Gabe repeated it a dozen times, trying to break in as she spoke.

Slater tuned him out and did some research on his phone. There were a couple of houses for sale in the neighborhood, and one was having an open house on Saturday, hosted by a real estate agent who'd posted her portrait on the listing, smiling and wearing a red power jacket, standing side-ways with one arm extended, her thumb up. Slater coached Gabe with the details, and he ran through it a couple of times, reciting the address. He was sharp, Slater knew, and wouldn't screw it up.

They pulled up to the security booth at the entrance to Rolling Hills, and Gabe rolled down his window. Normally he spoke working-class but unaccented English—he'd spent most of his life in this city—but now he put on an exaggerated Spanish accent and recited the address Slater had lifted from the real estate listing.

"Your name?" the guard in the booth asked.

"Eduardo Carrera," Gabe said.

The guard tapped at his keyboard and studied the computer screen. "You're not on the list," he said finally.

"No one put me on the list because no one is living in the house," Gabe said. "Miss Jennifer from the real estate company hired me to paint. She's doing an open-the-house on the weekend. I'm painting the front, outside only. The color is Italian cream with Covina taupe on the trim."

"No one told us about that," the guard said, frowning.

"You want I should call Miss Jennifer?" Gabe waved his cell phone. "You can talk to her."

"No," the guard said, glancing at the growing line of vehicles accumulating behind Gabe's truck. He tapped at his keyboard again, then said, "I guess it's OK. I'll have to copy your license, and your friend's." Leaning down to peer at Slater, he called to him, "Sir, what's your name?"

"His English is not so good," Gabe said, and turning to Slater, gestured impatiently and said, *"cédula."*

Slater pulled out his wallet and fished for his ID, and Gabe handed over both of them— Eduardo Carrera's Missouri driver's license with Gabe's photo, and a card with Slater's face on it, labeled REPÚBLICA DE HONDURAS: REGISTRO NACIONAL.

"Does Mr. Moreno have a U.S. ID?" the guard asked.

Gabe looked at Slater, who sat their impassively, then turned back and said quietly, "No."

The guard sighed and made a photocopy, then handed the cards back. The arm blocking the road swung up. Gabe shifted into gear and headed onto the quiet private street.

"That was fun," he said.

"I just wish Miss Jennifer would get her act

together and put us on the list," Slater said.

Gabe guffawed, and Slater looked at his phone to give him directions to Gil Martinson's address. They wound their way up through the plush neighborhood, passing horse fences and stands of open scrubland between the ranch houses, making a couple of turns but always heading uphill.

When they were close, Slater said, "Slow down, but keep moving."

The house was at the crest of the hill, and Slater studied it as they rolled past. It was big, sprawling even, but not palatial, and close to the street. That was probably compensated for by a big backyard. Unlike Gabe's house, there were no bars on the windows, no steel doors, and just a waist-high garden gate at the side of the structure leading to the back. That barrier across the road at the bottom of the hill and the uniformed guard in the little booth must provide enough security, or at least the feeling that they were immune from crime.

The three garage doors were closed, the driveway empty, but parked just past the house, pulled up tight to the bordering hedge—a ficus of some kind, maybe a Benjamin—was an old white Neon.

Around the next bend, Slater had Gabe pull over, then climbed out to peel off his coveralls, glad to be rid of them.

"Keep your phone on," Slater told him, and

walked back toward Martinson's house.

Past the driveway, in the strip of yard between the street and the front door, were three different hibiscus bushes, blooming enthusiastically, two of them red and one yellow. How did they manage to make those thrive up here? Rather than knock on the door, he went to the side gate and let himself in, walking around to the back.

The backyard was huge, with a swimming pool, manicured grass, and a breathtaking view of the ocean far below, dotted with freighters. A woman was stretched out on a chaise longue under an umbrella, wearing sunglasses and a bikini, an unbuttoned billowy top around her shoulders. She could definitely be Scandinavian, Slater thought, so pale and so blond.

She was absorbed in her phone but looked up at Slater.

"Are you here for Father?" she asked, seemingly unconcerned at his approach.

"If Father is Gil Martinson, yes."

"He's inside somewhere," she said, and then smiled.

She might have been flirting, but it was hard to tell behind the big sunglasses.

"Do you want some lemonade?" she asked. "It's fresh. From that tree over there."

"No thanks," he said affably. "What's your name?"

"Ahn-yes."

It took Slater a moment to realize it was a version of *Agnes.* It sounded much prettier without the hard *g.* Slater introduced himself, and Agnes set her phone face-down beside her on the chaise.

"Do you work for Father?" she asked.

"I'm doing some research on a former employee of his. I thought he might be able to enlighten me." He grinned at her. "You look like you're on vacation today."

Agnes pulled her glasses down for a moment, revealing tired red eyes with dark circles under them. "Recovering from a night out."

"I've been there, sister. The lemonade will help."

She picked up her highball glass and tilted it toward him, then took a sip. "So are you from the police?"

"I'm not a cop."

"You don't look like an office worker either. I'm thinking some kind of private detective. You're not a mobster, are you?"

Slater laughed. "I'm an investigator, and you're right, I work out in the field, not at a desk. I'm not connected to mobsters. What do you do? Professional socialite?"

"That's such a nice way to put it. Better than 'party girl.' I do have a career, though."

"Doing what?"

"I'm going to be famous."

"OK—famous for what?"

"I'm not sure yet," she said thoughtfully. "Singer, actress, fashion model. I've got some contacts. It'll happen."

"Lucky for you, you don't have to get a job in the meantime. You can just hang out here."

The glass door to the house slid open, and a guy stepped out, in his forties, maybe, with a bad haircut and an ill-fitting brown suit, open at the collar. He was holding a pistol in his hand.

"How did you get in here?" he demanded.

"Don't point your gun at me," Slater called to him.

He knew this guy—not personally, but he knew the type—too much of a bully or too stupid to make it into the police force, but from the way he was holding the weapon, finger away from the trigger, he knew what he was doing.

"Put that thing away," Agnes said. "We're having a conversation here."

He lowered the weapon but kept it in hand. "Who are you?"

"You must be Max," Slater said. "I'm here to see Mr. Martinson."

"You can't just walk in here and make demands like that. How did you get into the community?"

"He's not making demands, Max," Agnes said, her tone weary. "Tell Daddy he has a visitor."

Max reached into his jacket to holster his gun, then walked over to where Slater was standing, positioning himself between him and Agnes.

"I'm serious," Max said. "How did you get in?"

"We got off on the wrong foot," Slater said. "The name is Slater Ibáñez." He stepped toward him, reaching out to shake hands. Max didn't reach for his hand, instead looking wary, but Slater was close enough now to grab his wrist and spin him around. Max hadn't been prepared for that, and yelped in pain as Slater twisted his arm behind his back. He reached around into Max's jacket and snatched the pistol, then pushed Max hard, sending him tumbling onto the grass.

Looking at the weapon, Slater deftly popped out the magazine, then slid open the breech.

"There's one in the chamber, Max. You could have hurt someone."

Max stayed prone on the grass, watching as Slater snapped the loose bullet into the mag and then pocketed it. He tossed the pistol into the pool, where it sank fast, hitting the bottom with a muffled *clank*.

"Why are guys with guns so dumb?" Slater asked. "It's almost like there's something missing. Like they're trying to compensate for some inadequacy."

Agnes laughed, and Max stood up, finally, glaring murderously at Slater, and brushed himself off.

Another man appeared at the sliding door, maybe around sixty, with salt and pepper hair, a little mustache, and a pot belly visible under his bathrobe. Martinson.

"What's going on?" he asked.

"You have a visitor," Agnes said, "and he just schooled Max."

Slater put his hands on his hips and gestured to Martinson with his chin. "Why is your PA packing heat?"

Martinson frowned. "What are you doing in my yard?" His English was American, but slightly accented, the vowel in "yard" stretched out.

"Having a chat with Agnes," Slater said, "until your goon pulled a gun on me. I must say, sir, that your hospitality is sorely lacking."

Martinson grinned, and kept his eyes on Slater. "I told you I don't like those things, Max. Someone could have been shot. To whom do I have the pleasure?"

"Slater Ibáñez. I work for Cudahy Mutual Insurance. I'm looking into Jason Hughes's workplace injury."

"I don't know what I could tell you," Martinson said, taking a few steps toward him. "I barely knew the man, and I didn't see it happen. I'm sure your people have inspected the equipment he was using."

Agnes had gone back to her phone, Slater

noticed, and Max stood on the grass, red-faced at being disarmed but deferring to his boss.

"It was a ladder," Slater said. "I'm surprised you didn't know him, considering you only have eight employees."

"That's the magic of our technological era," Martinson said, a smile playing on his lips. "Labor costs are falling as automation allows us to maximize our profit margins." He gave Slater the once-over. "Although your job won't ever be automated, I suspect."

"In my experience, entrepreneurs tend to be control freaks. I'm surprised you're not down there more often."

"Mr. Goff takes care of my interests."

"Really?" Slater said, cocking his head. "Preston seems like a bit of a wet noodle to me. I wouldn't trust him with my business."

"Your business is probably more"—Martinson looked for the word—"animated than mine." He grinned. "I'm sure you have some stories."

"I guess everyone does."

"Would you like a drink?"

"Catalina made lemonade," Agnes offered, glancing up. She'd been paying attention after all.

"I was thinking something stronger," Martinson said. "Scotch, or bourbon?"

"Sure, I'll drink your booze," Slater said. "Either one is fine."

"Come inside," Martinson said, and stepped through the sliding door.

Slater looked at Max and raised his eyebrows. "After you."

Max glared at him and went inside.

"It was nice to meet you, Agnes," Slater said, careful to pronounce her name the way she had.

Inside was a sprawling rec room, the furniture all white and pale-blond wood, the floor white tile. Near the windows two puffy white sofas faced each other, separated by a low bamboo table. It looked more like South Florida than Southern California. Max stood near the doorway leading farther into the house, eyes on Slater, hands folded and back arched, like a pompous security goon at a nightclub. At least he'd found something to do that didn't involve fuming. Slater lingered closer to the sliding door to the yard, leaving it open.

Martinson went behind the little bar, fronted with bamboo, and set out two tumblers, then pulled out a bottle of scotch. Slater didn't know the brand, but the label declared it to be single malt.

"Catalina," Martinson shouted, turning toward the doorway where Max stood. "Bring me some ice."

"I guess I should ask if you want ice," Martinson said, eyeing Slater.

"Not in that stuff. I want to taste it."

Martinson laughed and poured them both

neat, handing one to Slater and then sitting on one of the puffy white sofas. He folded one knee over the other, and rested his arm along the back of the sofa cushions. Even in a bathrobe, Slater thought, he was the image of the boss.

Slater sat on the facing sofa, at an angle where he could keep an eye on Max, and sipped the scotch. It was smooth, and woody, and delicious, and he savored it on his tongue.

"From your expression, I see you approve," Martinson said.

"It's like mother's milk."

Martinson threw his head back and guffawed, then sipped his own drink. "I can taste that too."

A woman appeared in the doorway behind Max, ignoring him and pushing past. Squat and dark, with her hair bundled neatly behind her head, she was wearing a black-and-white maid's uniform, and carried a silver ice bucket in both hands. This must be Catalina, Slater realized. He'd been in houses with staff, but he'd never seen anyone in the full-on traditional uniform, and he gaped at it as she entered.

"Ice?" Catalina said, approaching the sofas.

"I don't need it now," Martinson snapped, scowling at her. "Leave some in the fridge."

"Yes, sir," she said meekly, and went behind the bar. Slater could hear her transferring the ice into another container.

"So—about Gislitech," Martinson began. "I don't have to go in to the office because so much of the work is automated. I communicate with Mr. Goff regularly, so I'm able to work from here. Who wouldn't choose this view over a desk in that building?" He gestured languidly toward the yard, ignoring Catalina as she walked past Max and out of the room. "Controllers are high-tech, but they aren't really that complicated, and as other technology changes dramatically, controllers change only incrementally. Most of the work is done in China, of course, and our responsibility here is shipping parts to customers …"

Slater half-listened, not trying to understand what he was saying about the business but assessing why he was saying it. He could have easily had Max give Slater the bum's rush, but maybe acting civil, engaging with him, boring him with these pointless details was a more effective way to ensure he'd stop nosing around. He let Martinson rattle on for a while, then sat forward and drained his glass.

"Thanks for meeting with me, Mr. Martinson. I'll be in touch if I need any further information." He stood, and Martinson rose with him, following him to the door to the backyard. Before he stepped outside, Slater turned back and looked him in the eye. "I forgot to ask: what can you tell me about the Indians?"

Almost imperceptibly, Martinson's easy expression hardened. "What Indians?"

"You know: in Calexico."

Martinson shrugged. "I don't know what you're talking about."

"You were detained at the Calexico border crossing. Surely you remember that."

He gestured helplessly. "A mix-up with my green card. It took a while, but eventually I got it worked out."

"All right," Slater said. "Thanks for sharing the good scotch. I'll find my own way out."

Agnes's chaise was abandoned, the yard now empty. At the bottom of the pool Max's weapon was a wobbly black stain. Slater walked out through the side gate and onto the street, then past the front of the house, again admiring the hibiscus. The white Neon was still parked against the ficus. It wasn't Agnes's or her father's—neither one would be caught dead driving something so old and worn, he was sure of that—and a guy like Max probably had wheels with way more horsepower. Catalina's car, he decided.

As he passed the Neon, behind him he heard rapid heavy footsteps approaching, too close now even to turn around to look. He ducked into a crouch just as Max took a swing at him. He heard the whiff of metal in the air over his head, and the momentum of the missed blow sent Max stumbling over Slater's back, rolling onto the street, the shovel he'd been wielding clattering to the asphalt. Slater scooped up the ersatz weapon and aimed at the blade at Max's face.

"A shovel?" he demanded. "You were going to crack my head open? What kind of an animal would do that?"

He held it there, inches from Max's neck, until he was certain the guy would stay down, despite the red mist of rage in his eyes. Stepping to the side of the street, he thrust the blade into the earth beneath the hedge and left it there, the handle standing erect. Max started to get up.

"Don't you fucking move," Slater growled, but Max was already on his feet.

"Goddamn beaner," Max snarled, and rushed at him, throwing a punch, which Slater easily dodged.

"Whoa—racist too. You're the whole package," Slater said, and lunged toward him, throwing a quick left, connecting sharply with his cheek. Max spun around, catching himself from falling but looking disoriented. The guy knew how to handle a firearm, but knew nothing about fist-fighting.

"Why do you make me do this?" Slater shouted. He fended off Max's lame attempt at another blow, then hit him again, hard, in the face, spinning him the other way. "Why couldn't you just let it go?"

Max stumbled toward him again, clearly punch-drunk now, and Slater grabbed his shoulders and kneed him in the gut, hard enough to wind him but not enough to do any damage. He pushed Max to the pavement—he was headed that way anyway—gasping, his face contorted.

"Fucking idiot," Slater muttered, watching for a moment to make sure he'd stay down, then walking up the street. Gabe was waiting in the truck with the windows rolled down. He'd changed out of his coveralls. When he saw Slater approach, he sat up, shooting him a questioning look as he climbed in.

"Drive," Slater said grimly.

They drove past Max, on his knees in front of the white Neon, trying to catch his breath.

"Is that your doing?" Gabe asked, slowing down and rubbernecking.

"Don't ask."

They rolled past Martinson's house. Around the next curve, strolling on the side of the street in flip-flops, was Agnes, now wearing a sarong, holding her phone languorously.

"Slow down," Slater said.

"Beautiful woman," Gabe said quietly.

"Really? I hadn't noticed."

Gabe cackled. "Bullshit."

He rolled down the driver's window, and

Agnes looked in, pulling up the brim of her floppy hat.

"There you are," she said.

"Walking off the hangover?" Slater asked, leaning toward Gabe.

"I was hoping to catch you. Can we talk?"

Either she hadn't seen Slater's altercation with Max, or she was remarkably sanguine about it, Slater thought. Either way, talking with her might give him a chance to ask her about her father's affairs.

"Sure," he said. "I don't think Max wants to see me back at your house. Can you come down the hill with us? There's a coffee place on PCH."

"In a work truck?" she said, and then smiled. "What an adventure."

She padded around to the passenger's door, and Slater opened it for her, sliding over to the middle of the bench seat and flashing Gabe a grin.

"What did you want to talk about?" Slater asked, his hands between his knees, once they were headed down the hill.

"I thought maybe I could hire you."

"I only do corporate jobs," Slater said.

"It won't take long. I just need someone to come with me to a meeting. You're the kind of guy no one is going to mess with."

"What kind of meeting?"

Agnes leaned forward and glanced sidelong at

Gabe. "I'll tell you at the coffee place."

Gabe sighed, and Slater directed him to a strip mall along the highway. He parked near the coffeehouse, and the three of them climbed out.

"Maybe you could go get a coffee," Slater said to her. "I'll just be a minute. Do you need some cash?"

"I have my phone," she said, waving it.

"Order me a double espresso."

"How does it work?" she asked. "Is it like a restaurant?"

"Not quite. You just walk up to the register and tell them what you want, and they'll tell you what it costs. After you pay, they bring the drinks to the other end of the counter."

"Awesome," she said, and flip-flopped leisurely toward the shop.

"She's never been to a counter place before?" Gabe asked, watching her walk away.

"More likely her wealth has sheltered her from doing things like ordering her own coffee," Slater said. "Listen, I don't want you to wait for me—I'll take a ride-share back. What do I owe you?"

"Well," Gabe said, folding his arms and looking thoughtful, "it's about twenty-five miles each way, plus my time. Plus the risk of using the fake ID. Plus memorizing the story of Miss Jennifer. Plus the stress of giving a ride to a rich girl."

Slater laughed, and waited for him to think it

through.

"Maybe three hundred?"

"Done, my friend," Slater said, and pulled three C-notes from his wad of cash.

Gabe thanked him and climbed in his truck, and Slater walked into the coffeehouse. Agnes was just sitting down at a table by the window. In her clueless helplessness she'd managed to get one of the staff to wait on her, a gangly teenage boy who brought over a foam-topped mug and a little espresso cup, setting them on the table. Agnes thanked him, flirting a little, touching his arm. The kid beamed as he walked away. With her sunglasses off, she looked tired.

"I never come in here," she said, as Slater sat down. "It's cute."

"Your friend Max seems like a bit of a hot-head," Slater said, sipping his espresso.

"He's not my friend. I don't know why Daddy keeps him around."

"I had to school him again before I left."

She chuckled. "I wish I'd seen that."

"He seemed pretty upset," Slater said. "I hope he doesn't escalate and come after me. He might get hurt."

Don't worry about him. Daddy will keep him in line."

"What do you know about Daddy's business?"

"Nothing," she said flatly.

"There was mention of the Indians when he was detained at Calexico."

"I don't know anything about that," Agnes said impatiently. "I wanted to ask for your help with my thing."

Slater leaned back in his chair, cradling his little cup. "All right. What's your thing?"

"I have to go meet a guy in Hollywood tonight and buy something from him."

"Why do you need me to come along?"

"I don't trust him."

"You think he might try to rob you."

"Exactly," Agnes said, nodding.

"What are you buying?"

She took a deep breath. "Well, we used to date, and he took some raunchy photos of me."

"And you're paying him to delete them? That's blackmail, and it's illegal. You should go to the cops."

"I know it's illegal, it's just … it's easier this way. If I call the cops, he'll distribute the photos, and that will damage my career."

"Lots of people have become famous because of raunchy videos," he said. "Maybe it would actually help with your career goals."

"They're not just sex photos. There's more."

Slater nodded, waiting for her to continue.

She looked at her cup. "I know him, and I know he's not a bad person."

"But he's blackmailing you, and you don't trust him to keep his word. Why do you believe that he'll delete the pictures?"

"He's going to put them on a flash drive for me. That's why we have to meet."

Slater frowned. "Just because they're on a flash drive doesn't mean there are no other copies. How much are you paying him?"

"Ten grand."

"Seriously? That's a lot of scratch."

Agnes shrugged. "So will you come with me?"

"Why not? I'd love to rough the guy up a little. It sounds like he deserves it."

"Don't do that," she insisted, "unless it's absolutely necessary."

"Tell me about this guy," Slater said, draining his little cup.

"We met at a club, in Hollywood. He works there." She smiled sadly. "He's not even a bartender—he's, like, an usher."

"Do you know if he carries a weapon, like Max?"

"No way." She shook her head. "He's not a thug. Although I didn't expect him to shake me down either. I guess I should just say I never saw a gun."

"If you give me his name, I'll look him up before we meet him. Maybe I'll learn something useful."

"How cool," she said, swirling her cup. "You have access to a criminal database?"

"Something like that," Slater said, and pulled out his phone.

"His name is Eric Reyes, and he lives in Atwater, in someone's garden house."

"Do you know his date of birth?" Slater asked, thumb-typing as she spoke.

"No idea," she said, but then added, "wait—I do. It's four twenty, the same as for pot. But I don't know the year. He's about thirty."

"What time are you meeting him?"

"Ten o'clock tonight, in front of the Egyptian Theater."

"That's a public place," he said, looking up at her, "and there are always lots of people around, so it should be safe enough. Give me your phone number." Slater typed as she recited it, then texted her. "Did you get my message?"

She looked at her phone and said, "Got it."

"On the boulevard, near the theater, right on the next corner, there's a souvenir shop. Text me when you get there, and we'll meet inside, before we go to the Egyptian."

She grinned at him. "How can you remember what stores are there?"

"There's a souvenir shop on every corner for a mile," he said. "So this trash bag wanted cash?"

"Correct."

"Let me carry it," Slater said. "I'll do the hand-off."

"Good idea. I should bring enough to pay you as well—how much do you charge for doing something like this?"

Slater hadn't even thought of that, and he dropped a number that seemed absurd, just to see what she'd say. "Two grand."

"So I'll need twelve thousand. Note to self," she said, looking at her phone and typing.

Slater couldn't help but grin. This was going to be easy money.

"Is there anything else we need to discuss?" she asked, looking up at him.

"I met Catalina earlier. Does she live with you?"

Agnes looked confused. "She lives in Carson, I think. Why?"

"Just curious. Does she make you dinner, or does she go home before that?"

"Weekdays she works noon to seven. She cooks in the evening, but she doesn't make lunch. Why is that important?"

"It's not," Slater said, waving dismissively. "As far as Eric is concerned, I think I've got what I need."

"Then I'm going to get a car," she said, pushing her cup aside and returning her focus to her screen.

"I'll do that too," Slater said, and summoned one on his own phone.

Agnes seemed to feel no social pressure to talk anymore, and remained absorbed in the screen. Arms folded, Slater watched her, fascinated by her unself-consciousness.

"Mine's here," she announced finally, and Slater followed her outside.

Agnes waved at a black town car that was moving slowly in the parking lot, accelerating toward her and gliding to a stop when the driver spotted her. He jumped out and stepped around to open the door. Agnes waved good-bye to Slater as she climbed in behind the tinted windows, in her natural element, the black-uniformed driver gently closing it behind her.

Slater's ride-share appeared a few minutes later, a little silver Prius. Most people rode in the back, but Slater climbed in the front. It was easier to keep an eye on the driver, and less obvious to anyone else what their relationship was. His driver, an absurdly pregnant woman, was dressed more down-market than Agnes's—she wore a stretchy pink top that barely covered her belly, and her arms were a distracting riot of colorful tattoos. Slater had her drop him at a Blue Line metro station in Long Beach. Even though he was likely coming into some cash tonight, he couldn't afford to take a chauffeured ride all the way home at rush hour. The train moved faster at this time of day anyway.

It was crowded, and he had to stand, hanging onto the overhead bar and swaying with the train's motion. He noticed a Latino kid with spiky hair sitting nearby, gazing absently at Slater's pants. When their eyes met, Slater was grinning, and winked at him. The kid turned red and looked away. No way was he going to hit on a teenager, but if the kid was interested in his crotch, Slater wanted to encourage him, show him that there was nothing wrong with that. But the kid was embarrassed now, studying the floor, and as other commuters pushed their way in and streamed off, Slater soon forgot about him, lost in his own thoughts.

Goff and Martinson were both hiding something, he was sure of that now. And Max—hopefully he'd settle down. No amount of skill with his fists was any match for Max's bullets. He wasn't going to worry about it, though. He'd dealt with smarter punks than him.

O N THE WALK from the metro station to Gabe's block, he paused at a quiet street corner that had a wide sewer grate. Looking around, and satisfied that he wasn't being observed, he pulled out Max's mag, wiped it down with his hankie, and dropped it into the sewer.

The Thunderbird was where he'd left it, and once he'd climbed in, he checked Conrad's whereabouts on his phone. He was at home, not at work. Freaking idiot. Why couldn't he be where Slater needed him to be? He sighed and started the ignition, pulling into the street. It meant he'd have to go to Agnes's meeting blind. There were records that he could check into himself, but only if he had precise information, like a Social Security number and a birth date. Otherwise it was next to impossible. For Conrad, though, using the databases the police had, not having those details wouldn't even slow him down.

Conrad. Slater knew what he was doing at home, out in the fucking Valley—sitting on his ass playing video games like a teenager. Knowing him, he was probably fucking someone else, some twinkie, or some other cop, or some twinkie cop. The thought of it was infuriating.

The car in front of him was still stopped, the driver spaced out, even though the light had turned green, and Slater honked. A frail hand appeared above the seat, waving in apology, and as she turned the corner, Slater saw that she was elderly, and tiny, blotchy bony hands on the steering wheel, barely able to see over it. He felt a pang of guilt. How low was that, picking on an old woman?

Still in Gabe's neighborhood, rolling past a *pupusería*, he realized he was hungry. They made some here with just beans and the *curtido*, he knew, and checked the time on his phone. If Catalina worked until seven, he definitely had time to eat first. He circled the block and parked out front, then went in to eat at the counter, savoring the delicious tortilla, hot and fresh. The flavors and the heat of the spices were intense enough to push the frustrating thoughts of Conrad right out of his mind.

The last thing he wanted to do was get on the gridlocked freeway and drive back to the fucking South Bay, but that's where Catalina was. Traffic wasn't as bad as he'd anticipated, though, and eventually he was parked across the road from the entrance to Rolling Hills. Looking at his phone, there were a couple of ways out of the neighborhood, but if Catalina was headed back to Carson, this would be the one she'd use.

If Martinson was always as brutish with her as he had been when Slater was there, he suspected she probably wouldn't linger at work, and sure enough, not long after seven, the little white Neon rolled down the hill, pausing at the gate for the arm to swing up and waiting at the intersection to turn right. Slater started the Thunderbird and pulled into the traffic, whipping an illegal U-turn when he could, hoping no cop had seen him do it.

Catalina wasn't an aggressive driver, and that car wasn't capable of moving very fast anyway, so he hung back, keeping her in sight a few vehicles ahead. She made her way into a residential neighborhood, tract houses from the 1960s or maybe the 1970s, Slater estimated, spaced close together and within a few blocks of the 405 freeway. It was still a reasonably decent neighborhood, though, without security gates and bars on the windows, although the cars in the driveways implied the residents were working-class.

Catalina pulled into a driveway and climbed out, still wearing her black-and-white uniform, a bulky shoulder bag in one hand. Slater parked at the curb a few houses back and watched as she went inside. He'd give her a minute, he decided, and pulled out his wad of cash, folding up a few individual twenties and a hundred so they'd be easy to palm.

When it had been long enough that she wouldn't feel like he was stalking her, he walked up to the house. The lawn was green and tidy enough to golf on, and under the front windows was a bed of black *Aeonium*, the thick petals of the rosettes at knee height. Someone had tended these properly, pruning the ground-hugging stems and encouraging the others to grow upward into a lush even row. The purple-black succulent grew all over the place, but it was pleasing to see them well tended, a nice accent to the tan-stuc-coed house.

Catalina pulled open the inside door when he rang the bell, leaving the screen between them. She'd changed into a blouse and pants, and she frowned when she saw him, but then he saw a spark of recognition.

"We didn't actually meet," Slater said, "but I saw you today at Gil Martinson's house."

"I remember," she said neutrally, her English

lightly accented, and folded her arms, waiting for him to continue.

"I'm an insurance investigator, and I'm looking into Gil. I wonder if I could ask you a few questions."

She watched him for a moment, and then broke into a smile. "You took away Max's gun."

"I did," he said, grinning back at her. "I thought he was being quite rude, waving it around."

"Mr. Gil is in trouble with insurances?"

"Maybe," Slater said. "I'm not sure yet. I know he works from home, but does he go out sometimes?"

She looked wary, but said, "Sometimes."

"What kind of car does he drive?"

"Max drives, and Mr. Martinson sits in the back. It's a Bentley."

Of course he had a freaking Bentley.

"A new one?" Slater asked. "What color?"

She frowned. "You're working on car insurance?"

"In a way," he said, and dug out one of the folded-up twenties, flashing it so she could see what it was and then pushing it between the screen door and the jamb.

Catalina unlocked the handle and let the door open a crack, plucking the bill from his fingers. It disappeared into her pants pocket.

"It's brown," she said, meeting his eye, "with

sparkles in the paint."

"It would really help me a lot if I knew when Martinson was going somewhere in that car." Slater pulled out a business card and slipped it beside the screen door, holding it there until she took it. "If he was headed out, you could just text me something like, 'leaving in twenty minutes.' I'd be very grateful."

She looked dubious, but Slater produced the folded-up C-note, the zeroes plainly visible, and passed it through the door. Catalina palmed it without hesitation.

"Give me as much advance notice as you can," Slater said, his tone businesslike now that the deal was sealed. "You can send a second text just saying 'now' or something, so I know that's the moment he's driving away."

"I'll try."

"I hope so." He smiled sweetly. "If you forget, I know where you live."

She flinched, but Slater didn't wait for her to respond, stepping away from the door and heading back toward the street.

"*Gracias, Catalina,*" he called to her, waving as he strode back to the Thunderbird.

She'd follow through, he knew, partly because of his vague threat, partly because he'd paid her to, but mostly because she almost certainly hated Martinson. Slater hated him, and he'd only met him for a few minutes. But it had been long enough to see how he treated people.

———◦———

TRAFFIC HAD EASED UP by the time he got on the freeway again, and he made it home with only a slight delay, in the perpetual congestion on the 110 downtown. Once he was upstairs he grabbed his laptop and stretched out on the sofa, instead of pulling out the bourbon, which he knew was still waiting patiently for him in the kitchen cupboard. One of his booze rules was that he wouldn't have more than one unless he was with people or he was in for the night, and he'd already had one with Punch-face Martinson.

There were too many people with Agnes's ex's name to find his address, but he found a social media page for an Eric Reyes that was publicly visible. It felt like it might be the right one because it mentioned club land, and specifically venues in Hollywood. If this was the guy, he looked like a punk. His profile photo showed him with a premium bottle of champagne, his lips planted on the label.

It didn't seem like Slater should be tired, but when he set the laptop on the carpet, frustrated with the fruitless search for Eric, sleep soon pressed down on his consciousness, insisting that he close his eyes. Before he let it overwhelm him, he set the alarm on his phone to wake him in time to go meet Agnes.

———◆———

HOLLYWOOD WASN'T FAR, AND he knew where he could usually find street parking, especially on a weeknight, and pulled up to an open meter on a side street a few blocks from the Egyptian Theater. On the walk there, he smelled night-blooming jasmine on the muggy evening air. There was nothing quite like it, the intoxicating signature scent of a summer night. He looked around for the bush, but he must have passed it already, or maybe it was behind a fence.

His phone buzzed with a text, from Agnes:

I'm here.

When he got to the boulevard, Slater looked in the souvenir store on the corner, then the one next door, and then the one across the side street, where he finally located Agnes. Even though it was well after dark, she had on her big sunglasses, and pulled down over her brow a blue ball cap with the interlocking letters LA. But the straight blond hair was unmistakable. She was flicking through a rack of T-shirts, wearing a colorful top, ragged jean shorts, and red cowboy boots.

She looked up as he made his way between the piles of screen-printed cotton, postcard racks, and shelves of mugs. "You're wearing the same shirt."

"I usually stick to one wardrobe change per day," Slater said.

Agnes pulled her shoulder bag around and took out an oblong object wrapped in a red handkerchief.

"Here's the ten," she said, passing it to him and fishing in her bag again.

"It's a bundle of hundreds?" he asked quietly.

"Correct. And this is yours." She handed him a thin white business envelope.

Slater could feel the thickness of the cash inside, and didn't bother to open it, folding it in half and stuffing it in his back pocket. Glancing around to make sure no one was watching them, he undid his belt buckle and stuffed the handkerchief bundle down the front of his pants.

"Ew," Agnes said, wrinkling her nose.

"Eric's not going to mind," he said. "We should go—if we get there first, we have the advantage."

"So professional," she said, weaving through the store's narrow walkways and leading him out to the street. "I'm glad you know what you're doing."

It was just a few steps to the courtyard of the Egyptian Theater, a movie palace dating to the 1920s and modeled after the ruins at Karnak. Faux sandstone walls painted with murals of the ancients and their hieroglyphics lined the little space, and queen palms towered overhead. A few people were lounging on benches in the courtyard, and a couple of tourists were admiring the artwork, but it wasn't crowded the way it would be if a movie were about to start.

"He's not here yet," Agnes said, looking around.

"We'll stand on this side," Slater said, selecting a spot with a good view of the entrance and the rest of the space. "When he gets here, let me do the talking."

"Fine," she said, fidgeting in her boots and looking around. "Thanks for being here."

"It's my job," he said, and they stood in silence, both of them watchful.

Agnes looked at her phone. "He just texted. He says, 'Come to the parking lot.' What do we do?"

Slater thought about it, putting his hands on his hips and looking toward the walkway that led back to the parking, past the empty box office at the side of the theater. Eric was clever to summon them there. In the middle of a movie screening, it would be full of cars but not people—no witnesses.

"We'll go," he said finally. "You walk out first, and I'll catch up when he shows himself."

Agnes murmured agreement and headed

toward the walkway.

Sure enough, when they got there, the parking attendant's booth was dark and abandoned. Those guys closed up shop and left the gate open when the lot filled up, which would have happened much earlier in the evening. Agnes wandered between the cars, looking around. Farther back, a vehicle flashed its headlights, and Agnes walked toward it.

Slater caught up to her as she reached the vehicle, a black Audi. Eric stood beside the driver's door. It was the same guy he'd found a photo of, kissing a bottle of champagne. His dark hair was gathered in a topknot and he had a carefully trimmed beard. He was a little paunchy, Slater saw, and thick, but it didn't look bad on him. If that was his car, Eric was definitely earning more than a busboy.

"You brought a damn cop," Eric said, eyeing Slater suspiciously.

"He's not a cop," Agnes said, stopping a few feet away. "He's a friend. For security."

"I'm hurt that you think there's any reason to be afraid of me, baby."

"Of course I'm afraid—you're blackmailing me, you asshole."

Eric frowned. "Such ugly words. We're just conducting a business transaction. Where's the cash?"

"No way," Slater said. "Give her the flash drive first."

"The ape-man speaks," Eric said, raising his eyebrows. "First, show me the money."

Slater shook his head. "That's not how this is going to go down. Give her the flash drive, or we walk."

"So bossy," he said, and looked from him to Agnes. "All right," he said finally, and pulled a little black object from his pants pocket, tossing it to Agnes.

She examined it briefly and dropped it into her bag.

"You've deleted all the other copies of the photos?" Slater asked.

"That was the agreement."

"Then we're done. If you ever contact her again, I'll make sure you get busted for trying to blackmail her."

Eric frowned, and looked at Agnes. "You still owe me ten grand."

"You've already given her the photos," Slater said. "Why would she pay you now?"

"Because I'll email the photos to Daddy, and put them all over the Internet. Think about it, dog."

Slater stepped up to him and slapped him roughly, on one cheek and then quickly again on the other with the back of his hand.

"I am not your dog," Slater said intently.

Eric looked shocked, and held his hand to his face. "What was that for?"

"You still have copies of the photos."

"Of course," Eric said. "Do you think I'm stupid?"

"Yes, I do, Topknot," Slater said emphatically. "Now that Agnes knows your game, why would you expect her to pay you anything, ever?"

Eric's eyes hardened, and without another word, he climbed into his car and started it, revved the engine, and backed out, roaring out of the parking lot.

When he'd gone, Agnes pulled off her sunglasses and stepped over to Slater, punching him hard in the shoulder. "You big dummy."

"Ow," he said, rubbing his arm. She had surprisingly sharp knuckles. "Why am I dumb? He's the idiot—I just exposed his game."

"If you'd paid him, he wouldn't distribute my photos," she said, insistent.

"But if you paid him, he'd ask for another ten grand next month, and again the week after that. You'd never be free of it."

"I'm not free of it now either, am I," she demanded.

Slater sighed and rubbed his eyes. This was why he hated doing personal jobs. He reached down his pants and pulled out the red handkerchief bundle, handing it to her.

"Can you hang onto that for now?" she said. "It's been in your crotch."

Stuffing it back in his pants, Slater tightened his belt and said, "I'll walk you to your car."

They walked back toward the theater court-yard.

"I'm not driving. I'm using a car service," Agnes said, calmer now. "I might go clubbing."

"Do *not* go to the place where he works."

"I won't. So what was that double-slap thing you did? It was loud. He looked pretty surprised."

"It's called a kovac," Slater said. "It doesn't really hurt. I use it to get someone's attention. I learned it from a Russian guy. In Japan it's called *oufuku binta*, a round-trip slap. I heard an Irish-man call it the paintbrush, and a cop I know called it the Joan Crawford, because she used to do that in her movies, apparently."

Agnes looked at him askance. "You're like the Rosetta stone of interpersonal violence."

Once they were near the boulevard, she stopped inside the gate to the sidewalk and turned to him. "Thanks for trying, Slater. In some way I think you're right—at least now I know he's a liar."

"You know, I might be able to shut him down completely," Slater said, putting his hands on his hips.

"You're going to lean on him?"

"I don't think that would work with a guy like him. He has a very short attention span."

"Please tell me you're not thinking of doing something violent."

"Not physically. Just financially," he said. "I'm not sure I'll be able to pull it off, so no promises. You said he lived in Atwater—do you have his address?"

"I've been there with him, but I never wrote it down," she said, shrugging.

"You said it was a garden house. How does he get in? Does he have to walk past the main house?"

"We went in the back gate, off the alley. His door is right there."

"What does the gate look like?" Slater asked.

"It's redwood, and maybe about as tall as you are. The top is curved." She mimed the shape with one hand.

"Good memory," he said, and grinned.

"It's a nice alley too, not gross and dirty like downtown. Are you going to visit him?"

"You don't want to know that," Slater said. "If anyone asks you later, you can tell them the truth: 'I don't know.'"

She nodded. "That sounds smart. Do you need more money?"

"The two grand you gave me is enough to start. I'll let you know if it takes more work."

"Well, you can deduct it from the ten in your underpants."

Slater nodded. "Don't give Eric anything, and do not talk to him until you hear from me."

"Yes, sir," she said, giving him a mock salute, and then grinned. "Do you want to come with me to Cielo? It's just down the street. I could get you past the bouncer, and buy you a drink."

"Thanks, Agnes, but I only date guys."

"I'm not asking you on a date, you big mook. Just for a drink. I can get you into places you normally couldn't go."

"So you want me to be your bodyguard."

"You are such an egomaniac," she said, exasperated. "Why are guys like that? Gay, straight, it doesn't matter—they're all puffed up." She pulled off her ball cap and adjusted her hair, ruffling it with her fingers.

"I can't answer that," Slater said, "because I'm not a scientist. Why are you going clubbing on a Tuesday night, anyway? This afternoon, you were still recovering from last night."

"I have to go out on weeknights. Saturday is amateur night."

Slater grinned. "I've heard that said before— usually by hard drinkers."

"Do you want the hat?" she asked. "I can't wear it out, and it won't fit in my bag."

He took it from her and tried it on, then

adjusted the strap to make it bigger, and pulled it onto his head.

"Very dashing," she said, appraising him, then added, "Good night, Slater," and walked out to the boulevard with a wave.

Slater went the other way, onto the side street and back to his car. Once he was behind the wheel, he checked on Conrad. He was still at home, the useless fucking idiot. Researching Topknot would have to wait until tomorrow.

When he got home he hung Agnes's hat on the back of the door, then opened the kitchen cabinet to find the bourbon. Just the sight of the heady amber liquid made him start to relax, and he poured a tumbler almost full, emptying the bottle, and dropped an ice cube into it.

Remembering the brick of cash in his pants, he loosened his belt and pulled it out, untying the handkerchief to reveal a stack of new hundreds, still wrapped in a yellow currency band. He never saw this much cash all at once, and he fanned through it with his thumb to make sure it was real. Agnes was either very trusting to leave it with him, or rich enough not to miss it. Tying it up again, he thought about where to put it. He should hide it, he knew, and he had a reinforced locker in the garage, but it was unlikely anyone would rob this place. He pulled out the kitchen junk drawer and stashed it under the clutter of ancient take-out menus at the very back.

Carrying his drink over to his recliner, he got comfortable and pulled out his phone, checking the hookup app to see who was nearby, swiping through a few faces and torsos and other body parts. Sex then bourbon, he'd thought on the way home, but now that he was comfortable, he realized he was tired. It shouldn't be a surprise: he'd been running around half the damn county today, dealing with Goff, and Martinson, and Catalina. Goff telling him he needed a shrink, that was rich. And worse, Doris and that fucker Albert. He killed the app and put on a *Sasquatch Search* podcast, drinking deeply and relishing the burn, stretching out in the dark, getting lost in the forest as the questers went deeper, among the redwoods, sinking into sweet oblivion.

SEVEN

LATER WOKE UP in bed, naked, his clothes dumped in a corner. He tried to remember getting here. He was almost certain he'd been alone. When he sat up, his head throbbed, but not too badly, and it subsided after a while.

On the kitchen counter sat an empty bourbon bottle, and beside it another one with a surprising volume already missing. Scowling, he looked in the fridge and found a bottle of orange juice. Had he bought that? It smelled OK, and he drank from the bottle, then put it back. He made a coffee and sat in his recliner, finally able to focus, and looked at his phone. It was still morning, he saw, and for that he was grateful.

First he checked the tracking app for Conrad's whereabouts. At work, finally, the dumbass.

He'd been at his station since before eight. Slater got dressed and pulled on Agnes's blue ball cap as he went down to his garage, where he unlocked the reinforced cabinet that sat in a corner at the far end, past the nose of the Thunderbird.

It was really a gun safe built to look like an ordinary storage cabinet, but Slater didn't have any guns, and instead used it to store stuff that he didn't want to get stolen, or even get seen: all his surveillance tools and electronics. Pulling open the heavy door, he found the gear he'd need, dropping it into his satchel along with his key set, a black vinyl zippered case with hundreds of door keys arranged in clear little pockets, dozens on each sheet, all of them numbered. The Russians had promised him these would fit ninety percent of the locks he'd encounter, and so far they'd been right. The key case made his satchel unpleasantly heavy, but if things went well, he'd need it today.

Climbing into the Thunderbird, he backed into the alley and drove the short distance to Conrad's station. When he phoned him, it went to voice mail, so Slater called the station's main number and asked for Conrad.

"You know I'm working, right?" Conrad said when the call was transferred to him.

"Oh, good," Slater said. "I'm right outside. Can you come out for a second?"

"No. I'm busy."

"I'm sure your union insists that you get breaks from time to time. It won't take long. I'm already here."

Conrad sighed audibly, for Slater's benefit, he knew.

"Give me a minute," he said, and hung up.

Slater got out of his car, lingering on the accessibility ramp, admiring the delicate blossoms of the globe mallow and waiting for Conrad to come out. When he did, he seemed aggravated.

"You know I don't actually work for you, right?"

"I can pay you, if you want," Slater said.

"I can't take your money," he said, shaking his head in disbelief. "Jesus, that's so corrupt."

"It's one simple thing. All I need is this guy's address."

"Fine. Text me the details."

"And also whether he has any criminal record," Slater said quickly, and pulled out his phone, thumb-typing a note to Conrad:

Eric Reyes, lives in Atwater Village, DOB 4/20/??

"When did you become a baseball fan?" Conrad asked, calmer now.

"You mean the hat? Someone gave it to me."

"You look hung over."

Slater looked up from his phone. "Fuck you very much."

"When's the last time you ate something?"

"I had some fruit for breakfast, and I have food in my car."

"Vegan Pop-Tarts don't count as food."

"You were entitled to care about that before you dumped me," Slater said, his voice rising. "Now you're just wasting your breath. You've already kicked the trash to the curb, man. Let it go."

"You're not trash, Slater. You know you're not. I want you to take care of yourself. I know that you know you should." Conrad held his gaze. "I know you try sometimes, at least until you get home at night. I know it worries you too, even though you'd never say that."

Slater put his phone in his pants and crossed his arms, swallowing before he spoke. "You're the only person who sees right through me," he said quietly. "The only person who knows what I really am." Slater studied his face. "And you don't want me."

Conrad was breathing hard. "I'll get back to you about your target," he said, and turned to go in.

Why had he ever let himself fall for this guy, let himself be so vulnerable? He remembered the feeling of Conrad's fingers in his hair, the warmth of his breath on his neck.

Slater closed his eyes for a second, clearing his

head. "Make it snappy, toots," he called after him. "I need to work on it today."

Conrad didn't reply, and pulled open the door, disappearing inside.

Back in his car, Slater started the engine to get the air-conditioning working. Scrabbling around in the backseat, he found a ripped-open box of Pop-Tarts, and ate one, then grabbed his tablet. He started a new file, titled "Agnes Martinson," and made some notes about meeting her, and the parking-lot encounter with Eric.

Glancing up when he saw movement in front of the police station, he saw Conrad step out and lean against the side of the building, looking at his phone. Such a beautiful man. The longing made his heart hurt.

His phone rang—it was Conrad.

"I'll text you this guy's street address," Conrad said, "but I wanted to give you a rundown on his rap sheet, because there's a lot to it."

"He's a bad boy?" Slater asked.

"Not really. You do much worse stuff before breakfast lots of days. You've done worse to me personally."

Slater scoffed, and watched Conrad, talking animatedly, unaware that he was being observed.

"He was arrested half a dozen times, assault and petty theft, and once for stealing a car. He's only had a couple of misdemeanor convictions.

Do you need those details?"

"I just wanted a head's up in case he's violent."

"Simple assault while under the influence is the only evidence of that," Conrad said. "He looks cute in his booking photos. Are you going to take him a corsage on your date?"

"The only date he has is with my fists."

Conrad laughed. "Go easy on him. Anyway, I should get back to work." But he stood there, grinning, listening.

"Are you at your desk now?" Slater asked.

"Yeah, I'm staring at a stack of paperwork, and the boss is floating around. I can't just drop everything whenever you need someone to hold your dick while you pee."

"I'll let you get back to it, then."

Conrad ended the call, and stood up straight, smiling to himself as he went inside.

Slater sat there for a minute, staring at the doorway, lost in thought. Conrad wasn't completely disinterested in him, it seemed. Maybe there was still a spark.

His phone buzzed with a text. It was from Conrad, sending Eric's address. Slater grinned as he shifted into gear and drove away.

———·———

ATWATER WASN'T FAR, JUST across the river, and Slater had soon navigated to Eric's street.

The garden apartment was attached to the main house's garage, which opened on the alley, and because it was a corner lot, from the side street he could see the gate Agnes had described. This was definitely the place: Eric's Audi was pulled up sideways, tight against the garage door. It probably wasn't a legal parking spot, but it was closer to his apartment than parking on the street. He must really value that car.

Slater circled the block and parked on the side street in a spot with an optimal view of the garden apartment. From here he had an eye on the car, the redwood gate, and the tops of two of Eric's windows above the fence. But the car was probably an easier way to keep track of him, he realized, rather than doing full-on surveillance, as Eric wasn't the kind of guy who'd walk anywhere. Slater could come back later to check for the Audi. The idiot worked nights, he knew, so he might not even wake up until the afternoon.

But then he saw movement in one of the windows, the pane sliding open, or maybe shut. Slater reached for his binoculars and checked, zeroing in on it. It was definitely closed now. Then Eric emerged from the gate, wearing douchebag satin gym shorts and a T-shirt with the sleeves ripped off, still with the topknot. Slater instinctively slouched down, watching as Eric climbed into the Audi and pulled out of the alley, driving right past him toward the boulevard.

Slater reached into the floor of the backseat and found the box of black latex gloves he kept there, snapping on a pair and then climbing out of the Thunderbird, pulling his satchel onto his shoulder. Walking toward Eric's gate, he scanned the street for observers. A gardener pushing a noisy mower was the only person in sight, farther down the street, and he clearly wasn't interested in Slater. Scanning the alley for video cameras, he couldn't see any, but he pulled the bill of his cap down over his eyes anyway before he reached over the redwood gate to unlatch it.

Eric's front door was out of view of the main house, behind a hedge, some kind of juniper that looked like it was getting too much water. Planting it there was understandable; the homeowners had probably got sick of seeing the tenants' comings and goings, and put it in for their own privacy. There were no cameras in sight here either, and Slater checked the door handle. It turned freely, leaving only the deadbolt preventing him from entering.

Reaching into his satchel, he pulled out the key reader—a handy little device that was essentially a probe at the end of a length of wire that plugged into his phone. Slater started the app, which had everything written in Cyrillic, except the important part: the key numbers. Sliding the probe into the keyhole in the deadbolt, he twisted it slowly around, until the screen on his phone went green and listed three numbers. He was happier when it only picked one, but three wasn't a huge waste of time.

Squatting on the doormat and glancing over his shoulder, he pulled his key case from his satchel and zipped it open, then flipped through the heavy sheets until he found the key with the first number on it. He stood up and looked around, and satisfied that he was still alone, tried the key in the deadbolt lock. It wouldn't budge, even when he wiggled it around, so he crouched down again and replaced it, then flipped to the sheet that held the key with the second number. This one worked, easily turning the bolt, which slid open with a satisfying *thunk*. He slipped the key into his pocket and zipped up the key case, stuffing it into his satchel again, and then, wiping his feet on the mat, pulled the door open.

There was no alarm, thankfully—that would have instantly ended this visit—and he stepped inside. A quick look around revealed it was mostly one room with a kitchen at one end, a lone bed-room off to the side. The layout was like his own place, but with luxe-looking kitchen stuff, and a lot cleaner. It was also completely uncluttered, like it had been prepped for a real estate photo shoot. The windows faced the yard and the main house, but no one would see him from there, as the curtains were drawn. Eric's laptop sat on the kitchen counter, folded open, but the screen was dark. There was no stool to sit in front of it, and the counter was too high to use one of the chairs from the dining table. Did Eric stand here to use it? What a freaking weirdo.

Slater fished in his bag for the electronic gear he'd need—first a USB dongle, inside a zip-top plastic bag so that it wouldn't get lost. It was matte black and so thin as to be imperceptible, unless the user happened to need that USB port and found it blocked. He pushed it into Eric's computer, using the port marked with a power symbol so that it would work even when the computer was sleeping, feeling it click into place.

The relay unit was a bigger piece of hardware, disguised to look like a transformer for some portable device. That was a canny design choice, Slater thought, as it needed to plug into the wall. He looked under the kitchen counter for an open socket, then examined the microwave above the stove. Microwaves were usually plugged in, not hardwired, and the socket was often out of sight behind the unit, or in a nearby cabinet. Sure enough, the socket for this one was in a high cupboard that held only the exhaust fan's ductwork and a couple of empty plastic take-out containers.

Slater reached up and plugged the relay unit

into the other socket, and watched the indicator lamp. First it lit up in red, and then it turned amber. That meant it had successfully connected to the USB dongle he'd put in Eric's computer. A moment later it turned green—it had also connected to the cell network. Slater grinned. He loved those Russians. Now he could be anywhere and see every keystroke Topknot typed.

Closing the cupboard door, he pulled on his satchel and scanned the room, making sure he hadn't disturbed anything or left any gear. On the way out he locked the front door with his ghost key and scanned the yard, then the alley as he went through the gate. When he was back on the street, he took a deep breath, feeling his whole body relax: no one had seen him. He peeled off the black gloves and stuffed them in his satchel, wiping his hands on his jeans to dry off the sweat.

There was a great bakery near here, he knew, that had vegan cheese, and he drove to the boulevard and parked out front, then sat inside to eat. He checked the keystroke surveillance app, but nothing had happened, and it showed him the inscrutable message "нет активности." At the bottom, though, for some reason the notifications were in English, so he knew that it was "connected" and in "standby mode."

Closing that app, he checked on Conrad, who was still at work. What a goddamn fool, trashing

Slater's eating habits when he ate at those gross-out burger joints, and industrial tacos, whose main ingredient was sodium, from the late-night drive-through. Maybe Slater's food thing was high-maintenance, but at least he didn't eat whatever deep-fried trash was dumped in front of him.

After he'd eaten, as he was on his way out to his car, Della broke through his aggravation. Slater wiped the scowl off his face and answered her call.

"Preston Goff is none too happy with you," she said.

"I'm shocked to hear that," Slater said, hoping it was evident in his tone. "You know I have impeccable manners."

Della just cackled.

"When did he call you? I was over there yesterday."

"This morning."

"What did he say, exactly?" Slater asked, climbing into the Thunderbird.

"Nothing specific. Just that you were impertinent."

"Is that a real word?"

"It means 'inappropriate.' Did you hit on him or something?"

"I may have flirted a little—raised an eyebrow, that kind of thing," he said, and started the engine.

"Well, he was upset, and in a whiny kind of way."

"It sounds like he's getting worried, but he's afraid to make a formal complaint—especially if he waited twenty-four hours to call you. He's hiding something, Della, and I'm getting closer to finding out what."

"He wants you to stay away from Gislitech."

"How do you feel about that?"

"We've got something he wants," Della said, "not the other way around. Do what you need to do. If he squawks, I'll tell him to get back in line."

Slater grinned. "That's all I need to hear. Thanks for the head's up."

As he ended the call he saw that he had a text, from a number he didn't know, in area code 424. That was the South Bay—it had to be from Catalina. Her message was curt:

30

That meant Martinson and his idiot stooge were leaving home soon. Slater checked his navigation app. He could get there in time, if he hustled. Pulling onto the boulevard, he made his way to the freeway, accelerating up the ramp and heading south.

There was no guarantee Max would drive out the same gate where he'd seen Catalina yesterday, but it was the closest one to Martinson's house, so it seemed like a reasonable bet. Slater parked across the road from the guarded gate and waited.

It was only a few minutes until his phone buzzed with a text, again from Catalina:

Now.

Slater grinned and set his phone down to watch the gate. Catalina was definitely earning that C-note. It took Max just a few minutes to drive down the hill, and Slater slouched back instinctively when he caught sight of the Bentley, brown and sparkly, as Catalina had described, with Max's ugly mug behind the wheel. The side windows had a dark tint, so he couldn't see Martinson, but he knew he was in there—he could feel it.

Max turned left onto the main road, and Slater pulled into the traffic when he could. The Bentley was hard to miss, and he let it get some distance ahead of him, catching up each time at the next traffic light. The car went north on PCH, and it was easy to tail Max, as he was a calm driver, probably because his boss was in the backseat. He kept to the left lane, and wasn't the type to punch it when confronted with a yellow light.

They were somewhere in Redondo Beach when the Bentley turned left, into a hotel parking garage. Slater followed, but had to wait for the next light. By the time he was pulling into the lot, the Bentley was headed out again. Max drove right past him without even glancing at Slater.

The most likely explanation for the quick turnaround was that he'd dropped Martinson here, and with any luck, Slater could catch up to him. Stopping at the valet stand, he handed over his keys, waiting impatiently for the guy to produce a claim ticket.

It was an upscale place, he saw, walking into the lobby. Slater didn't look too out of place, as even denim was considered dressy in LA, but still, he didn't want to bump into Martinson, so he stopped in the garage doorway, furtively glancing around. The target wasn't at the reception, where a couple of people were talking to a staffer behind the counter, and he wasn't lounging in the plush lobby furniture, which was nearly abandoned at this time of day. Maybe he'd gone upstairs to a room, Slater thought. But there was one other possibility: the bar.

Choosing a cushy wing chair that faced the bar, Slater dropped into it and pulling out his phone, pretending to be absorbed in it, but keeping watch on the entrance. He couldn't see much in the dark interior. From the configuration of the space, though, it was unlikely there was another way into the bar, unless it led directly from the garage. If Martinson was in there, he'd have to come back this way.

Slater did look at his phone as he sat there, casually checking on Conrad, still at his station, the idiot, and then messing around with the keyboard surveillance app. Eric hadn't touched his computer, but the app was still connected. He navigated the mishmash of languages in the menus, hoping the setting labeled NOTIFY was the right one to activate so that the app would alert him when the laptop was put to use.

The bar seemed quiet, and all the time he'd sat there, only a handful of people had come and gone. Some looked like tourists, and some like they were on a break from the office during the mid-afternoon doldrums. None of them, however, were Gil Martinson. Slater decided he'd give it a little longer, then go have a look inside before he left.

His hunch had been right, though, and Slater froze when he saw Martinson stroll out of the bar. He was wearing a white linen suit and sandals, a gold chain visible under his open collar. All that was missing to complete the Riviera look was a white fedora.

More interesting was the woman on his arm, dressed incongruously to him, in heels and a skimpy black cocktail dress. He had an arm around her waist, but they weren't talking. She was young enough to be his daughter, Slater thought, although unlike Agnes, she was dark, maybe South Asian, with a luxuriant and well-coiffed mane.

Martinson didn't notice Slater, sitting across the lobby, or even look in his direction. Instead he went to the reception desk and handed something across the counter. It was the size of a credit card, but from Slater's vantage point it was hard to tell what it was. The woman he was with stood back a little and casually scanned the room, her gaze landing briefly on Slater. Martinson scooped up the room key the clerk slid across to him, then turned around and took the woman's hand, leading her toward the elevators.

She had to be a prostitute. Who else would be hanging around a hotel bar dressed like that in the middle of the afternoon? And what was it about straight guys and hookers? Surely Martinson could find a damn girlfriend. Slater hated the sight of his face, and his instinct was to punch it, but he wasn't a bad-looking guy—most women wouldn't feel repulsed.

The desk clerk would probably tell Slater what room he'd rented, although it would cost him some cash to find out, given that this was ostensibly an upscale place. But there was really nothing to learn from following them up there, and Slater didn't give a shit about Martinson's sex life.

After he was sure they'd boarded the elevator, he got up and headed for the parking structure, digging out his valet ticket. What a waste of an afternoon.

EIGHT

HE JOB THAT had started all this, investigating Jason Hughes's insurance claim, needed some attention, so he headed toward Hyde Park, taking the advice of his navigation app to stay on surface streets and avoid the heavy congestion on the freeways. It was still daylight, and Jason knew what his vehicle looked like, so he parked around the corner in a spot where he could see Jason's stairs and the garage door.

Jason had a car, he knew, a little silver Chevy. It was probably in that garage under his apartment, because Slater had done a sweep of the neighborhood the first night he'd come down here and hadn't been able to locate it. The guy was home now, he knew, because the windows at the top of the stairs were open. If he'd gone out, he would have locked them, as they were on the landing and at waist height—an easy mark for an opportunistic passerby.

Surveillance always involved a lot of sitting around, sometimes followed by intense bursts of adrenaline-charged activity, sometimes not. Slater settled in, leaning back in the driver's seat, the windows cracked for ventilation, and kept an eye on Jason's stairs while he used his phone. Nothing from Eric's keyboard yet, and Conrad had gone home. Is that all he ever did, went home and went to work? Slater sighed. This might be a long evening.

The orange glow of sunset was bright in the sky—and Jason hadn't budged—when his phone beeped. Slater pulled it out to check. Eric was typing. Watching the screen, it was obvious he hadn't noticed the dongle. In the app, every keystroke ran together in one long string of seeming gobbledygook, and it was unclear what program he was even using, as it only showed what he pressed on the keyboard. It looked like he was writing an email, but that wasn't important. All Slater wanted was the first few characters that Eric typed—the password to get into his computer. With predictable finesse, Eric had chosen BALLER, all in caps.

Slater watched the streaming text for a minute, glancing up at Jason's place, and put the phone aside when he saw a blue Prius pull up at the bottom of his stairs. Jason soon appeared, walking down the steps one by one, favoring one leg. He was wearing jeans today, with his black brace tight around his left knee. As Jason climbed in the back of the car, Slater thumb-typed the time on his phone and then twisted the key to start the Thunderbird. He couldn't see the ride-share logo in the Prius's windshield, but clearly that's what the vehicle was doing, taxiing him somewhere.

When the car was halfway up the block, Slater pulled into the street to follow it. Traffic was heavy enough that he didn't have to rush or even concentrate to keep up to it, and when it turned onto the boulevard, he let a couple of cars get between them. Jason wasn't going far, however, and the Prius soon turned into a strip mall. Slater pulled into a street space just past it and watched in the rearview mirror as Jason climbed out and started up the stairs to the second floor. Slater couldn't see what business he went into, not from this angle, but the Prius hadn't waited for him. He pulled back into traffic and circled the block, parking on the other side of the street.

From here he could see the walkway along the entire second floor, which had a lawyer's office, a pot dispensary, something written in Korean, and Crenshaw Physio. He knew Jason was a pot head, but he also claimed to be injured. Had he gone into the physiotherapy place? If he had, it didn't mean the injury was legit, because Jason knew he was being surveilled—he could be doing it just for Cudahy Mutual's benefit.

It was a depressing thought, that people could be so devious, so corrupt, and Slater hated that he saw it in absolutely everyone, not just the fraudsters and the chiselers and the cons, but in people who were probably decent. It was a struggle just to keep an open mind when the default was suspicion. Jason might really be injured, he had to remind himself, no matter how much he wanted to punch his lights out.

Keeping an eye on the strip mall, Slater climbed out and fed the parking meter, then sat in his car with his binoculars. They revealed nothing more than he could see without them, so he set them aside.

Exactly forty-two minutes later, he noted for his records, Jason stepped out of the physiotherapy place and eased himself down the stairs, climbing into the backseat of a waiting car, a dark-red sedan. Why was he taking ride-shares when he had his own wheels?

Slater started the Thunderbird and pulled over into the central turn lane, then made a quick U-turn, gunning the engine in the brief break in the oncoming stream of vehicles. Jason's ride wasn't that far ahead, he saw. In the dense traffic he tailed it onto Florence, paralleling the metro tracks, and then into a commercial part of Inglewood, onto a street that seemed quiet considering the time of day.

The red sedan stopped in front of a row of shops, giving Slater enough warning to pull into a parking space before he passed it. The street had a lot of mid-century architecture, storefronts that still housed active businesses, but the gentrifiers hadn't been through yet, so the vibe was low-rent—wig stores, a smoke shop, a nail salon—dull and dusty and in need of paint. He watched from half a block away as Jason climbed out and hobbled into a doorway under a sign that read BETTY'S TAVERNA.

It looked like a dive bar, and there wasn't any foot traffic in and out from the nearly abandoned street, so there was no way Slater could walk in there without alerting Jason to his presence. Instead he stayed in the Thunderbird, one eye on the door to the bar, and added to his notes. If Jason planned on getting drunk, that could explain why he wasn't driving.

The last traces of twilight had gone when his phone beeped, and checking the keyboard tracking app, the first thing Eric typed, again, was BALLER. A few minutes later the typing stopped, and the app went into standby mode. Was Eric home for the evening? Last night the guy had set the meeting with Agnes for ten o'clock, which meant he'd probably gone to work from there. It made sense, as a nightclub wouldn't get busy until after eleven. Slater would wait until after that, he decided, then go to Atwater to see if the Audi was there.

A lengthy fifty minutes later, Jason stepped out of Betty's, accompanied by another guy, around the same age and dark, with little round glasses. He wore his hair slicked back, clearly as much a devotee of pomade as Jason was. Slater couldn't criticize—black hair was a lot of work, he'd been told. They looked happy, he thought, peering at them through his binoculars, but not too inebriated. Jason gave the guy a bro hug, which instantly got Slater thinking about what they'd look like naked in that position, and that made him hard. The friend was probably as much an idiot as Jason, but he wasn't bad looking. Given the right opportunity, Slater decided, he'd fuck him.

After the bro hug, Jason climbed into another car, and his friend turned and strolled down the sidewalk, away from the Thunderbird. Slater pulled his keys out of the ignition and waited, focusing on the guy as Jason's ride-share drove away. He went into a brightly lit bodega a few doors down from Betty's. People who were clueless about being watched made it so easy, he thought, climbing out and striding up the block.

As he waited outside the bodega, standing on the sidewalk, Slater checked his phone, and found that Eric hadn't used his computer again. Glancing up when the target came out of the shop, he saw that the guy was wearing a tight black T-shirt, but didn't really have any muscle definition, although his nipples were visible through the fabric.

"Hey—you're a friend of Jason's, right?" Slater asked him.

The guy stopped and looked him over. "Excuse me?"

Slater hated the way he said it, the way people always said that—it wasn't about not understanding, or not hearing; it was all about expressing indignation: "How dare you?" He forced himself not to react.

"I'm helping Jason with his insurance claim," he said evenly. "What can you tell me about his leg injury?"

"I don't know you," he said sharply. "I'm not going to tell you anything."

"You'd be helping your friend. I just have a couple of questions."

"Wait—you're the guy who was spying on him," he said, his eyes growing wide behind the little round glasses.

"Did he tell you that?" Slater said, putting his hands on his hips. "What else did he tell you?"

"He said you got a hard-on when you threw him against the wall."

"That's a lie. I never threw him against anything." Slater looked him over. "What I meant was, what did he tell you about his injury?"

"I'm not going to talk about Jason," he said, lowering his voice.

"And yet you're still standing here," Slater said. "What's your name?"

"Marcus," he said, and Slater handed him his business card. Marcus glanced at it and stuffed it in his pants pocket.

There was something in his expression, Slater thought, something that had shifted from his initial haughty disdain.

"I like your glasses," Slater said. "They bring out the color of your eyes."

Marcus laughed. "Bullshit. But thank you. See, I knew you were a man's man. Jason didn't quite get that, but I can feel it."

"Are you sleeping with him?"

"Dude," Marcus said. "He's totally straight. Not my type anyway."

"I get that," Slater said, thinking about it. He'd wanted to punch Jason almost from the instant they'd met.

Marcus took a deep breath and said, "So, I live right around the corner. Would you like to come over and, you know, have a drink?"

"I'd love to do that," Slater said, "but I can't."

"Are you married or something?"

"It would be a conflict of interest."

"What does that mean?"

"It means I have to keep my dick out of my cases."

Marcus nodded. "That's too bad. Maybe we could just, uh, say good night."

"Right here?" Slater asked, frowning.

But Marcus was already stepping back against the brick wall of the storefront, glancing furtively up the empty street. Slater moved toward him, standing close, gently tweaking a nipple, which made Marcus gasp, then putting his hands behind the guy's neck, leaning down to meet his willing mouth.

Not a bad kisser, Slater decided, although he moved too fast. Marcus tensed up for a minute as someone walked past and into the bodega, heels echoing on the pavement, but Slater didn't look, focusing on Marcus's mouth, arms encircling his shoulders, pressing his woody into the guy's belly. His hands were on the back pockets of Slater's tight jeans, gripping him through the denim, and Slater could feel him getting hard against his thigh.

"All right. I have to stop," Slater said, pulling back.

"You're sure you don't want to come over?"

Marcus said, his hand lingering on Slater's fore-arm, glancing down at his crotch.

"I can't." Slater grinned and gently straight-ened the guy's eyeglasses. Marcus really wanted him, and he could use that to his advantage. "If you helped me wrap up my investigation, though, there'd be no more conflict. We could have that drink, and then I could fuck you senseless."

Marcus caught his breath. "That sounds like extortion."

"Like I said, you'd be helping him." Slater put his hand on Marcus's cheek, stroking it with his thumb. Marcus closed his eyes and leaned into it for a moment, until Slater pulled his hand away. That must have done it, because Marcus sang.

"If you're trying to figure out whether Jason really got injured," he said, "I'm pretty sure he did. I know him from the service, and I trust him. I don't think he'd bullshit me. He said he fell off a ladder-type thing at his job, and they wanted to fire him as soon as he'd used up his sick days."

"Was he limping tonight, or has that gotten better?" Slater asked.

"I've only seen him a couple of times since his accident," Marcus said, frowning in thought. "He's wearing a knee brace, and favoring it a little, yeah. I think it's more about not putting weight on it, so that he isn't straining the injury."

"Did he say anything about the treatment he's

getting?" Slater had seen the medical report, and the orthopedic specialist's recommendations, but he wondered what Marcus had heard about it.

"He's supposed to do physio, and he said he went for a massage tonight, and spent time on the treadmill. The way I understand it, they can't operate, so he has to let it heal. Even so, it'll never be the same."

Slater nodded. That lined up with what he already knew.

"Jason is a decent guy," Marcus said. "He smokes a little weed, maybe, but he works hard and stays out of trouble. I don't think he's trying to play you."

"Thanks for your time," Slater said.

"So when will you be done with this case?"

"In a couple of weeks, most likely. You've got my number."

Slater kissed him briefly, then walked back to his car. As he navigated back to the boulevard, he passed Marcus, walking up the block.

NINE

ACK HOME, IT took a minute to store all his electronic gear and the key case in the cabinet in his garage. It wasn't long before he was going to drive over to Eric's in Atwater, but he had enough time to stretch out on the sofa and close his eyes, setting the alarm on his phone for eleven.

When it woke him, he checked the keyboard monitoring app and found that Eric hadn't used his computer again, so he headed out. This time he parked farther down the block, out of view of Eric's gate, and pulled on Agnes's ball cap and a pair of the black latex gloves before he climbed out, slinging his satchel over his shoulder. The Audi was gone, and Slater scanned the alley as he approached the gate, reaching over to unlatch it. He knocked on Eric's door, even though the windows were dark, and listened. There was only silence.

Wiping his feet, he used his ghost key to let himself in but didn't turn on the light, heading directly to the computer and waking it up. His phone beeped, making his heart pound, but then he realized he was tripping his own surveillance device. On the lock screen he typed BALLER, to make sure he was right about the password. Of course he was. It took a second to pry the dongle out of the USB port with his latex-clad fingernail, but eventually it popped out. He collected the relay unit as well and put both in his satchel, and stuffed the ball cap in too, running a hand through his sweaty hair and then drying his glove on his pants.

It was weird to be standing up to work a computer, but as he dug around, he soon forgot about that. Eric's laptop was as Spartan and well organized as his apartment. All the files seemed to be in a cloud storage account. A search for "Agnes" brought up a folder with dozens of photos in it, and Slater clicked on the first one, scrolling through the images. They were graphic nudes, of her alone and of Eric with her. The guy was smart—his own face was never visible, although his pudgy gut was unmistakable. Agnes was clearly aware of the camera, despite the raunchy goings-on. Why do people let themselves be photographed like this in the first place? He sighed and kept scrolling, until one of the images made him stop.

Agnes had a red handkerchief tied around her upper arm, a tourniquet, holding it with her teeth, and in her other hand a syringe, its needle painfully lodged in her arm. This was a lot more incriminating than the nudity and sex, especially if Daddy were to see it. If she was strung out on something, it also might help explain her lack of inhibition about the camera.

Slater found a flash drive in his satchel and plugged it in, copying everything in the "Agnes" folder and then deleting it from Eric's cloud drive. It took a few minutes, but he found the trash folder on the cloud and cleaned that out too, and the trash folder on the laptop.

Sitting there for a minute, staring at the screen, he thought about it. What if there were others? Looking through the cloud drive, he found three more folders with women's names, and one labeled "Kenny." All of them had methodically similar photos to Agnes's, with nudity, sex, and hypodermic use. Eric had photographed one of the women passed out, presumably from whatever he'd injected her with, the same red hankie in her hand. In the Kenny folder were images of a young man with a big nose and narrow-set eyes, his hair carefully coiffed. Clicking through the photos of Eric fucking him, Slater felt himself getting hard. There were syringe photos of Kenny too, the needle poised to slide into the skin of his inner thigh.

It wasn't just Agnes—Eric was running a blackmail factory. Standing there at the kitchen counter, he thought about it for a minute. In a way, it was none of Slater's business. Agnes had paid him to help out, so he was justified in erasing the images of her. Slater wasn't a cop, and didn't even consider himself a particularly principled person. Kenny and these women had known what they were getting into. But they were victims too, he decided, taken advantage of, disinhibited by whatever drug Eric had injected them with. He set to work, copying all the images to his own drive and then deleting them from Eric's and purging the trash folders.

Poking around for more, in another directory he found a folder labeled like the others with a woman's name, "Sofía." But this one contained no compromising photos, just a series of screenshots of emails and texts from Eric's phone. It wasn't a blackmail job, so there wasn't much point in going through it, Slater thought, but then a word caught his eye: Gislitech. He stopped and looked closer. It was in an email message, with Sofía's address in the "From" field at the top.

Don't mention Gislitech or any knowledge of
the company. She doesn't seem to be connected to her father's business, except as a benefi-
ciary.

She'd signed it simply "S." This was about
Agnes.

Slater went through all the screenshots, and
gradually came to an understanding of what Sofía
was all about. She was giving Eric tips about how
to woo "the woman," never named, but it was
clearly Agnes. Eric's responses contained questions for her: where to eat out with "the woman";
what a flattering little gift for her might be, considering she was wealthy. The time stamps on the
messages were spread over a couple of months,
and toward the end, things turned dark, with
Sofía admonishing him:

> Dumping her isn't what you were paid for, you
> little weasel.

Eric's reply was terse and final:

> *She* dumped *me*. Completely beyond my con-
> trol. Stop bugging me.

Next Slater scanned through the screen shots
of texts from Sofía. Not all of these were clearly
dated, some of them showing just the time of day,
but they read like she and Eric were collaborating
on stalking Agnes:

She said she's going to Cielo tonight. Look for her there.

Why had Eric kept such careful documentation of his conversations with Sofía? Slater stepped back, considering that and rolling his shoulders, which had started to ache from standing in the unfamiliar position. Eric had obviously been hired by Sofía to romance Agnes, and he was blackmailing her and several other women, plus Kenny. Was Sofía involved in all that? Sofía mentioned Gislitech as if that were part of the con, but she never mentioned any of Eric's other victims.

Change of plans, Slater decided. He needed to find out who Sofía was. Her email address was right there, and he wanted to search for it, but not using Eric's computer. He copied the Sofía folder to his own flash drive and then pulled it out.

There was another tool he could deploy so that he could poke around here later, and look at Eric's digital activities without coming back. In his satchel he found a different flash drive, this one bright red, and inserted it into Eric's laptop. A splash screen popped up: a menacing skull and crossbones labeled DEATH GHOST GANG REMOTELY MONITORING SOFTWARE in a graffiti-spray typeface. A text box below it asked, "To install on this device?"

Slater clicked "Install," and another box came up, instructing him to "Remove your flash drive." When he did, the screen briefly displayed "Poof!" and then disappeared. That was it. Those Russians were so good at this stuff. Now he could check back on Eric's tawdry chiseling remotely.

After he put the laptop to sleep, he looked around to make sure he'd left no trace of himself in the room, then carried his satchel back to his car, not bothering to put the ball cap on again, and leaving the door unlocked, the gate ajar. No one was on the street except a woman walking a little dog, farther down the block. He locked his satchel in the trunk of the Thunderbird and went back to Eric's apartment, where he turned on the lights. This wasn't a covert operation anymore—he needed to talk to the guy.

In the booze cupboard he found a beautiful unopened bottle of scotch, Glenferrick, a brand he didn't know, but it was twenty years old and single malt, which sounded impressive—and he knew Eric liked expensive booze. Checking the time on his phone, he knew that if Eric was at work, he wouldn't be back for hours. He found a glass in the cupboard, cracked the seal on the Glenferrick, and poured himself a healthy shot. Just one, he reminded himself, and he'd stick to that. Conrad was wrong about him having no self-control. In the kitchen sink he ran water over his gloved hand and shook a single drop into the glass.

Turning the lights out again, he settled into a comfy wing chair that faced the bed. Swirling his glass, he inhaled the exhilarating richness of it, then took a sip. It was perhaps the best scotch he'd ever tasted, certainly better than Gil Martinson's. The drop of water really did open it up. Taking his time with it was new, though—he enjoyed booze but never savored it. This stuff deserved the time to be appreciated.

———•———

DOZING IN THE CHAIR, the scotch long since consumed, Slater instantly became alert when he heard the redwood gate open and close, and then the front door. Eric was home, moving around, dropping things on the counter. Slater straightened up and waited for him, listening while he took a long noisy piss with the bathroom door open. The kitchen light went on, casting a bright square on the bed, and then off again. Finally Eric stepped into the bedroom, unbuttoning his shirt, and flipped on the light.

"Hey, Eric," Slater said.

Eric half yelped, half screamed, terror in his eyes. "What are you doing here?"

"We need to talk."

"You broke into my house?" Eric demanded,

anger overtaking his initial fear.

He stood there staring at Slater for a split second, and Slater knew what Eric was going to do before Eric did. He bolted out of the room, charging toward the front door. Slater was already on his feet.

"Come on, man," Slater said, and caught him in the middle of the living room by the back of his belt, twisting him around and slamming his back against the wall. Slater held his forearm against his neck.

"Don't you fucking move, or I'll crush your windpipe," he growled, and put his other hand on Eric's forehead, pushing his head back. The guy wasn't bad looking, despite the fear and the panting. That, plus the smell of latex, sweat, and Eric's flowery cologne, were turning him on.

Eric called his bluff, reaching up with both hands and jabbing his thumbs into Slater's eyes. Slater quickly slapped his arms away but lost hold of him. Eric ran toward the kitchen this time, no doubt to pull a chef's knife on him, the idiot. Slater grabbed his belt again as he passed the dining table and threw him to the floor, using his own mass against him to pivot his body while he swept his feet out from under him with his boot. Rolling him onto his back, Slater straddled him and slapped him hard, a powerful kovac, and then grabbed his wrists, pinning them to the floor.

"What did I say about not moving?" Slater shouted. "Why are you making me hurt you?"

Eric wriggled and struggled but then went lax, knowing he wasn't going to be able to break free.

"What do you want, man?" he whined. "I didn't even take Agnes's money."

"Information, Eric," he said. "It always comes down to information."

Watching him, Eric shifted his pelvis under Slater's weight, and his expression changed. "You've got a stiffy," he said. "You're enjoying this."

Slater frowned, not loosening his grip. "What's that got to do with anything?"

Eric shot him a sweet and sappy grin. It was easy to understand how he'd been so successful at wooing his victims, using this kind of charm.

"It changes things," Eric said. "Maybe we can have some fun, you and I."

"I thought your sex life was about extorting cash from women."

"That's business. This isn't," he said, pressing up into Slater's erection. "You're hot. I know you want me. I can feel it."

Slater watched him for a moment, then said, "I'll tell you what, Eric. I will fuck you, but if you try anything, or try to take off, I'll call the cops and blow your whole blackmail operation wide open."

"Deal," he said simply. "Are you going to let me go?"

"Is that really what you want?"

Eric laughed, and Slater released his grip, rising and standing back. Wary, he watched him get up. Eric pulled off his shirt then, and went into the bedroom. Slater followed, hesitating in the doorway.

"You want some of this?" Eric demanded, gesturing with a flourish to his pasty, flabby bare torso.

"Yes," Slater said, and then chuckled.

Eric frowned. "What's funny?"

"I like your confidence."

"Well, bring it on, big guy," he said, and sank onto the edge of the bed.

Slater unbuckled his belt, and remembering he was wearing gloves, started to peel one of them off.

"Wait," Eric said. "Leave those on."

Slater paused. "Oh, yeah?"

"Yeah—I'm a little kinky."

Slater left the gloves on and pulled off his shirt, then pulled his belt out of its loops and slowly coiled it around one hand. "This kind of kinky?"

"Yeah," Eric said, grinning and enthusiastic.

Slater pushed him face-down onto the bed and grabbed his wrists again, looping the belt around his upper arms and pulling it tight, fastening the buckle. Eric gasped as his elbows were forced together, pushing his chest out, his hands flailing. Flipping him over, Slater licked the hairy spot between his pecs and bit one of his nipples, evoking a yelp and then a moan. He grabbed Eric's topknot and roughly pulled his head around, locking his mouth on Eric's warm ready lips. Eric was a good kisser—Slater knew he would be—hard and soft and yielding in the right way. He tasted delicious, like yeasty stale beer.

Pulling Eric's trousers down around his knees, he exposed his engorged cock, which Slater squeezed, watching his ecstatic expression. He spent some time massaging a couple of fingers inside Eric, and had barely started to stroke his cock when Eric came, loud, his whole body spasming. What was it with these kids? Holding firm as Eric's orgasm subsided, he decided he was going to fuck him anyway.

"Condoms," Slater said.

"In the nightstand drawer," Eric said, still breathing hard.

Slater spent some time working his way inside him, with his fingers and then with his cock, getting more turned on with Eric's visceral reaction.

"Can I undo your topknot?" Slater asked, speaking softly in his ear, his arm gripping tight around Eric's chest.

"Why?" Eric asked, breathing hard.

"I want to, you know, play with your hair."

"Go for it."

It was held together by a little elastic band, and Slater pulled it off, breathing in the scent of it as it came loose. Wrapping a hand around Eric's throat, turned on by the throbbing of his pulse, he thrust faster and harder, and it took him a while, but eventually he came, straining deep inside him, his nose buried in Eric's hair.

Afterward Slater rolled onto his back to recover, and peeled off the condom and the latex gloves, dumping them on the floor, then put his arm over his eyes.

"Maybe you could undo your belt?" Eric said. "I'm sure I could wriggle my way out of it, but it's easier if you do it."

"I forgot," Slater said, and sat up to untie him, then gently massaged Eric's upper arms where the belt's stiff vinyl had chafed and made the skin red.

"You're very sweet," Eric said, watching him.

Slater grinned. "That's not something I hear every day."

"Do you want a drink, or some weed? I've got some vodka open."

"Nah, I'm good," he said, releasing Eric's arms.

"You know, I don't actually know your name."

"It's Slater."

"How did such a Latin-looking guy get such a waspy name?"

"How did a cracker with a Latino surname get to be so racist?" Slater demanded.

"I'm not racist."

Slater sighed, and put his arm over his eyes again. "My father was Latino, but my mother's Jewish. She picked my name."

"That means you're Jewish too."

"Technically, yes, I am."

Eric's palm made a gentle circle on his belly. "You should go to the gym. In six months you'd be perfect."

Slater chuckled. "That sounds like excellent advice."

"So how come you didn't pull a gun on me?"

"Why would I do that?"

"Guys like you usually pack heaters."

"It sounds like you're typecasting again."

"Is it because you were in prison? Felons can't carry guns, right?"

Slater moved his arm and looked at him. "I'm the one who's going to ask the questions."

"Of course," Eric said, still massaging his belly. "What's she paying you? Did you get the rack?"

"What rack?"

"The rack—the ten grand."

"What did I just say?" Slater said sharply.

"Right, right."

"I'm not here about Agnes. I want to talk about Sofía."

Eric's hand froze, and then pulled away. "What about Sofía? Did she send you?"

"Tell me who she is."

"If you don't already know her, let me tell you now, you do not want to mess with that woman."

"I'll decide that."

"I've only met her a couple of times," Eric said.

"I know she hired you to get close to Agnes, so you know her that well, at least."

"Who told you that, if you don't know Sofía?" he demanded.

"Who's asking the questions, Topknot?"

Eric rolled away, onto his back, sullen now.

"Say it," Slater said, raising his voice.

"You are," Eric said, not looking at him.

"We can do this the easy way or the hard way. I don't want to hurt you, Eric, but I will if you make me."

"You're such a bully."

Slater rolled toward him and wrapped his hand around his throat, right under the jaw where it hurt but didn't impede the airway, and squeezed until it was comfortably tight. Alarmed, Eric reached up and grabbed Slater's arm with both hands, but he knew better than to struggle. Slater could feel the sweaty rough beard under Eric's chin.

"I am not a bully," Slater said tersely.

"Dude, chill," Eric said, his voice distorted by

the pressure, fear in his eyes, gently pulling on Slater's arm.

Slater let him pull his hand away, but he stayed in the same position, watching him, his palm on Eric's chest.

"I don't know how Sofía found me," Eric said. "Maybe through someone I work with at the nightclub. She came in there and asked for me by name, bought me a beer. When we met, she knew that I run the business with the photographs."

"How would she have heard about that?" Slater asked.

"The only people who know about it are the women themselves. Maybe it came from one of them." Eric grinned, remembering, already forgetting Slater's fingers around his throat. "Some people don't care about sex photos. They want copies to send to their friends and their publicist. Others are willing to pay to keep them suppressed."

"Did she tell you to blackmail Agnes?"

"That was just the gravy. All Sofía wanted was for me to get close to Agnes. We never got to the next phase, whatever that was. Agnes dumped me."

"What do you think the next phase was?"

"I have no idea. Maybe it was about extracting information." He mimicked Slater, deepening his voice: "'It always comes down to information.'

I thought there was something odd about the whole scheme, because Agnes doesn't have a job, or do much of anything."

"She's working on her career," Slater said. "Becoming famous."

Eric scoffed. "Her and every other idle trust-fund party airhead in this town."

He manipulated Slater's hand and laced their fingers together, resting them on his chest. Watching him, it seemed completely sweet and guileless, Slater thought.

"You know," Eric said, "it could have been about her father. Sofía told me to play dumb about him. Maybe she planned to get her hands on Daddy's money somehow."

That checked out with what he'd found on the computer. It didn't mean Eric was being up front about everything else, but at least some of it was true.

"How do you contact her?"

"Text and email," Eric said. "She usually phoned me."

"You don't know what she does, or where she lives, or who she works for?"

"I don't get paid to ask questions."

"Why are you afraid of her?"

"I made her pay me in advance, and I didn't complete the project. I'm afraid she'll want her money back."

There was more to it, Slater suspected, but he didn't press him.

"Get me her contact info."

Eric disengaged his hand and rolled over to pick up his pants and extract his phone, swiping and tapping at it, then showing it to Slater, who grabbed his own phone and copied the number.

"Why do you prey on these people?" Slater asked, setting his phone aside. "Sex is one thing, but hooking them up with drugs?"

"Agnes showed you the photos, huh."

Slater raised his eyebrows, waiting for him to continue.

"The dope was nothing to do with me," Eric said. "I just got lucky that I saw it, and could photograph it."

It was a lie, Slater knew. All the women and Kenny had been photographed with the same kind of syringe and the same red tourniquet.

"I wouldn't have pegged Agnes for a junkie," Slater said.

"She's not—at least not yet. Agnes is one of those people who claims to be a casual user. I only saw her do it a couple of times."

Slater watched as Eric spoke, letting him elaborate, spin out the lie. He was pretty convincing—but then, in his line of work, he had to be.

"Is that even possible?" Slater asked. "Doing it once in a while without getting addicted?"

"The way I understand it, there's only two possible outcomes. You stop, or it kills you."

Slater rolled onto his back and covered his eyes again, thinking. "Maybe it's like squatchers."

"What are squatchers?"

"People who search for the sasquatch. Some of them get really into it, and it kind of takes over all their free time. They're always out in the woods looking for giant footprints and scat, listening for the sasquatch's call. It's not really bad for them, right, as long as they can do their regular jobs and pay the rent."

"Huh," Eric said dubiously. "I don't think injecting smack is quite as easy on your system as a walk in the woods." He was quiet for a while, and then sat up. "Are you going to stay? I want to have a shower."

"I'll go," Slater said, and got up, taking the pile of wet latex to the kitchen trash, then coming back to get dressed.

Eric stood beside the bed, watching him, his hair falling around his face. "That was a lot of fun. Maybe we can hang out again sometime."

"Maybe," Slater said, sitting on the wing chair to pull on his boots, taking a long critical look at Eric. There was definitely potential with this guy for more than sex. But he was the wrong kind of bad boy, Slater decided: sleazy, and exploitative, and a really good liar.

"I'll let myself out," Slater said, and walked out to his car.

When he got upstairs to his apartment his eyes locked on the bourbon bottle—the mostly full one, not the empty—sitting on the counter. Could he have just one more drink tonight, just one drink right now, even though he was in for the evening? He dumped the empty in the trash and filled a tumbler from the other bottle, taking a deep initial gulp. He checked the time on his phone. It was so late, and he needed to sleep. Standing at the counter, he slammed the contents of the glass, then poured another. He wasn't going to find out anything about a one-drink limit tonight.

TEN

HIS MOUTH WAS dry and tacky when he woke up. After he drank the last of the orange juice from the bottle in the fridge, he stooped to look inside. Besides the can of instant coffee, there was a jar of pickles and a couple of little take-out containers of salsa. He pulled out the coffee and microwaved a mug of water, mixing in the powder and swirling it around with a spoon.

In his recliner, watching the strip of pale-blue sky through the dusty window, he sipped at it, remembering the night before, what Eric had told him about Sofía, and having sex with him. There was no danger that he'd fall for a guy like that, he knew that now, and even though Eric had potential as a fuck buddy, he was an unapologetic con artist, and inevitably Slater would get caught up in it somehow. No, he was done with Eric.

Pushing it out of his mind, he drained his mug and found his phone, then checked on Conrad's whereabouts. Zooming in on the map, he saw he was at a big-box store in the Valley. Obviously he wasn't working today, the goddamn slacker. What did he need at a bulk store, anyway? He lived alone, and didn't eat anything that couldn't be micro-waved or handed out a drive-through window. Closing the app, he tried to forget about Conrad. He did not want to start the day in a bad mood.

Looking around for his laptop, he found it under the sofa, and sat down again to search for Sofía's email address. He didn't even need Con-rad's help, it turned out, because Sofía had used her work email to communicate with Eric—the search brought up her company's website. South Bay Provisioning, it was called, and there was a photo captioned "Sofía Wallace, president," with a link to her email underneath. In the photo, she was standing in front of a cube van, smiling, arms folded—a professional photo, like the ones real estate agents used. Sofía had a chubby moon face, black hair curling around her head, and bright red lipstick. She was on the far side of fifty, Slater estimated, or maybe older, if this photo had been retouched.

The company's website was bare-bones, explaining little beyond "A family business providing quality goods and services at the Port of Los Angeles for over three decades." Slater did a Web search, asking "What does provisioning mean?" Reading the answer that came up, he realized Sofía's business had to be about selling supplies for the crews on cargo ships.

If Sofía was the president, she'd probably be at work today. Slater folded his laptop closed and went into the bedroom to get dressed. Halfway down the stairs, he remembered Agnes's cash. If he was going down to that part of town anyway, he really should return it. He trotted back up and retrieved the brick from the kitchen drawer, dropping it into his satchel, still wrapped in the handkerchief. Thinking about Sofía, he had a hunch about what she was up to, and retrieved one of his Russian electronic devices from the cabinet in the garage, setting it on the passenger seat before he backed the Thunderbird into the alley.

South Bay Provisioning was in San Pedro, not far from the port amid a long row of industrial spaces with razor wire–topped fences around the lots, and heavy trucks everywhere. The name of the business was painted on the bare metal fence, along with the street number, in fading black lettering. That had been there for a while—maybe the website's claimed "three decades" of history was legit.

The gate to the business was open, but Slater parked farther up the block, and picked up the surveillance device. It was thin and black, about the size of his phone, with heavy magnetic strips on one side. The power switch, as the Russians had shown him, was hard to see, recessed along one edge. It took a little fiddling with a fingernail to slide it on, but he knew he'd managed it when an indicator lamp next to the switch flashed green and then went out. As he climbed out of the car, he slid the device into his pants pocket, then walked toward the gate.

The site looked like a warehouse, with a loading dock and enough room out front for a big truck to back in comfortably. There wasn't one here now, just a couple of the cube vans Sofía had posed with in her online portrait, emblazoned on the side with SOUTH BAY PROVISIONING. Beyond the warehouse, at the far end of the building, was an office door with an awning over it, and he headed toward it, walking past the loading dock.

The door on the dock was rolled up, but no one was around. Several pallets sat just inside, recently unloaded or ready to be transferred onto another vehicle. One was stacked with boxes with air holes in them, each labeled ONIONS, and another had corrugated boxes with a canned soup logo on them. A third pallet was stacked with boxes marked GARBANZO BEANS. Slater stopped short, staring at them. There were two of those sitting in the Thunderbird's ashtray.

In the periphery he saw movement, toward the end of the building. It was Sofía, he could tell, even from this distance, her shape and the cloud of black hair unmistakable. In her portrait she'd been wearing work clothes, but now, improbably, she was dressed up, in a black pantsuit with a colorful pin. He strode toward her. When she gestured with the keys in her hand, the pickup truck she was headed toward chirped and flashed its lights. *Perfect,* he thought—she was leading him right to her car. Slater trotted to catch her before she climbed in.

"Sofía," he called. "Hold up."

She stopped beside the pickup, frowning suspiciously. "Do I know you?"

"Not directly," Slater said, "but we have mutual acquaintances."

"What can I do for you? I need to get to a meeting at the port."

"Selling food to shipping companies, or stalking Agnes Martinson?"

Sofía didn't react, and said evenly, "I don't know what you're talking about."

Slater put his hands on his hips. "Yeah, you do. I need to know why you're interested in her."

"And who might you be?" she asked, cocking her head.

"An interested party."

"Working for … ?"

Slater waved his arm impatiently. "Agnes."

"Bullshit," she said, and stepped closer, shoving her face up to his. "Stay out of my business, cowboy, or I'll push your dick in."

Slater didn't flinch. "That sounds painful. You've got the nails to do it, though," he said, glancing at her manicure as she stepped back.

She pulled open the driver's door of the pickup, but she was still staring at him, curiosity burning.

"So," Slater said, affecting a chirpy tone, "let me give you my card, and you and I can have a chin-wag if you decide you want to talk about Agnes, and Gil, and Gislitech."

Stepping over beside the bed of the pickup, he pulled out the contents of his hip pocket, palming the tracking device and dumping his keys and business card onto the dusty pavement. Stooping to pick them up, he heard Sofía sigh in annoyance at his fumbling. Keys and cards in hand, he moved toward her and gestured awkwardly.

"Can you take a card?" he said, thrusting them toward her and simultaneously resting his other hand on the side wall of the pickup's box, setting the tracking device under the lip, grinding his boot on the gritty asphalt so that Sofía wouldn't hear its magnets snap on as it attached. Sofía was engrossed in reading his card, however, and didn't notice what Slater's other hand was doing.

"Insurance?" she said, looking up at him with a sneer. "What does Agnes have to do with insurance?"

"I'm the one asking the questions," Slater said sharply. "Have you ever committed insurance fraud?"

"Get out of my place," she demanded.

Slater shrugged and walked away, toward the street, not looking back. Once he was through the gate, he flattened himself against the fence beside it. Moments later Sofía peeled out of the parking lot, moving fast, barely slowing to check for cross-traffic, and gunned it up the street, not even noticing him.

She was a tough customer, he thought, walking back to the Thunderbird. Not a civilian like Agnes, she swam in the cynical grimy depths with people like Slater and Eric. He knew the type, and he knew he'd never trick her or cajole her into confiding in him. He'd definitely managed to rattle her cage, though, which meant she might lead him somewhere interesting.

Once he was in the car, he glanced in the rearview, and satisfied he was alone, checked the app linked to the tracker he'd put on Sofía's pickup. It was only good for about eight hours, until the battery died, and less if she drove around a lot, as it was smart enough to conserve power when the vehicle was parked. But even a few hours might be enough to get a lead.

As he watched, the little red dot got on the Harbor Freeway. Satisfied that it was working, he closed the app, as he didn't have to see this in real time, and dialed Agnes.

"Please leave a brief voice message," her answering service told him. "Your message will be transcribed into text and delivered to this user."

"It's Slater," he told the machine. "I'm in your part of town, and I want to return something that belongs to you."

Back in the tracking app, he watched Sofía moving on the freeway, at "36 km/h." It was all in metric because the Russians who built this stuff were actually in Russia. He was fluent enough with kilometers to know it meant she wasn't moving very fast. That wasn't unusual, he decided. Traffic slowdowns could happen any time of day, for dozens of reasons—crashes, cargo spills, police chases.

His phone rang, and he picked up when he saw it was Agnes.

"So did you go see Eric?" she asked.

"Let's not talk about it on the phone," Slater said. "I'm in Pedro—can I come up to your house?"

"Not a good idea. Max is here, and he's black and blue because of you. Meet me at the coffee place."

Slater parked in the sprawling lot near the adjacent grocery store and walked over to the coffeehouse, finding Agnes sitting at a table in the corner with a foamy cup of something, and a little espresso cup waiting in front of the empty chair across from her. She'd dispensed with the dark glasses, wearing a colorful top and a very short skirt, her hair pulled back. More than she had before, today she looked wealthy.

"I remembered your drink," she said as he approached.

"Thanks." He grinned at her as he sat down. "Have you ever heard of someone named Sofía Wallace?"

"Never," Agnes said. "Who's she?"

"She hired Eric to pick you up and get friendly," he said, sipping his espresso and watching her closely.

"What?" she demanded sharply, and stared at him. "The whole thing was a setup?"

Her reaction was authentic, Slater decided—this was news to her.

"It seems that way," he said.

"I thought he really liked me."

"Maybe he did, later on, once he got to know you. But it didn't start out that way."

"Is this Sofía person in on the photo scam?" Agnes said.

Slater shrugged. "Maybe. If lowlifes know you

have money, they make you a target. I'm thinking that there's more to it, though. Maybe something to do with your father and Gislitech. I'm going to dig some more, and find out what her game is."

"Is she his girlfriend?"

He shook his head. "Just his employer."

"I'm glad now that I didn't pay him, the little prick." She stared out the window for a moment, blinking back tears. "It's so sad. He was such an attentive lover."

Slater frowned. "Really?"

"He knew exactly what I needed," she said, straightening her back and regaining her composure.

"Huh." Slater studied her face and sipped his coffee. He wouldn't have pegged Eric as particularly attentive. "Anyway, it's a good thing that you broke up with him. Don't have any further contact. If he bothers you, call me, and I'll deal with him."

"Sure," she said, "but he still has the photos."

"Maybe not. I managed to get into his cloud drive, and I deleted them there. I'm not sure if there are copies elsewhere. If he's smart, he'll have another backup. I'm not sure how smart he is. If he copies them to his cloud drive again, though, I'll know."

She stared at him. "How did you get into his stuff?"

"I'm not going to tell you that," he said, raising his eyebrows. "I did glance at the photos. The sex isn't really embarrassing, except that it's with Eric, and he's an ADD stain on our species. But I can see why you'd want the drug-use photos suppressed."

"Oh, god." Agnes rolled her head back. "I'm never going to do that again. He said smack makes you feel like you're flying, but I just got nauseous, and I had a three-day hangover."

"So the drugs were his?"

"Of course, Slater—do you think I'm a junkie? I don't even think he does it himself. In hindsight, it kind of came out of nowhere. I'm sure it was just a setup to take those pictures."

"That little fuck," he said, shaking his head. He'd known Eric was lying, but hearing it from her made it seem so much more malevolent. Why had he even slept with the guy, fallen for his charm?

"Don't go all paternal on me," Agnes said. "I already have a dad."

"It's not that. Listen, I have your handkerchief, and more importantly, what's inside it." Rising from his chair and meeting her eye, he said, "Don't worry—it's been sanitized. Let me get it from my trunk."

"Wait," she said. "You've done so much for me with Eric. Just keep it. If it's too much, maybe the rest can be like a prepayment, for future dealings with that pig."

Slater sank back into his chair. "If you can afford to part with it, I'll gladly take your money. Are you sure?"

She waved her hand dismissively. "You've helped me a lot. Maybe you can buy yourself a new shirt. That's the same one you were wearing two days ago."

Slater laughed. "It just looks the same. It's actually a different shirt." What he would invest in, he thought, is a brake job for the Thunderbird, and then maybe re-up on the surveillance tech from the Russians.

"Guys are so weird," Agnes said. "You need to hire a stylist. No one should ever wear the same thing twice in a week."

"Good to know," Slater said, and grinned at her. It wasn't every day he talked to a satisfied client, and this one had just dropped ten grand. "Can I drive you home?"

"Sure," she said, meeting his gaze. "As long as Max doesn't see you."

Walking outside, Agnes pulled on her dark sunglasses.

"Max shouldn't be mad at me," Slater said. "He needs to differentiate between business and personal stuff."

"You took his gun away."

"That was business. Then he tried to bean me from behind with a shovel. That's personal, and it's a big mistake. If you're going to be a bodyguard or work security, you need what the French call *sang froid*."

"I'll let him know," she said, grinning. "Why did you park so far away?"

"Just a habit," he said, and she waited while he moved things off the passenger seat into the back, then made a show of brushing off the seat for her.

"It seems absurd that a car this big only has two doors," she said, climbing in, "but it is pretty groovy. What's it called?"

"It's a Thunderbird."

"Is it older than me?"

"A lot. It's a '78."

"Does it go fast?"

He grinned. "Oh, yeah."

When he stopped at the gate at the foot of her neighborhood, the guard in the booth was the same guy he'd seen with Gabe, and he wondered fleetingly if he might be recognized. But the guy wasn't looking at Slater. Agnes pulled down her glasses, and the guard peered in at her, beaming.

"Hello, Ms. Martinson. Have a lovely afternoon," he said, and the barrier arm swung up.

Slater cruised up the hill and pulled into the driveway in front of her house. Catalina's little white Neon was parked in the same place against the ficus hedge.

As Agnes climbed out, she asked, "What was that French word you used?"

"*Sang froid*," Slater said. "You don't have to tell Max all that—it'll probably just make him angrier."

"It seems like you're better at it than he is, so maybe it'll actually help."

Slater grinned. "Sure. Maybe Max and I will go for a drink someday."

Around the first bend and out of sight below the house, Slater pulled over and shifted in to Park, but left the engine running. On his phone he checked on Sofía's location. She was on the freeway again, headed back toward Pedro at "89 km/h." But she'd made a stop, "16 м.," presumably meaning she'd been stopped for sixteen minutes, he decided. The dot on the map indicating the stop was way out on the southeast side of the map: Gislitech.

He dialed Agnes, grateful that she picked up.

"Did I leave something in your car?" she asked.

"No," he said, glancing at the passenger seat. "Is your dad home today?"

"I just saw him. He's dressed to go out, but he's still here somewhere."

"That's all I needed to know," he said, and ended the call.

Shifting the Thunderbird into Drive, he headed down the hill, fast, the big car hugging the yellow line. The navigation on his phone told him he could get there by three, and if Preston worked as hard as he claimed, he'd be in his office.

On the freeway his phone buzzed with a text, from Catalina:

20

She was a great informant, he thought. Martinson must be on his way somewhere. But he didn't have time for that now.

At Gislitech he walked in the front door, ignoring Karen Chen, and headed up the stairs behind her desk.

"Excuse me," Chen demanded, and then louder, "Stop."

Goff's office door was closed but not locked, and Slater went in without knocking. A black duffel bag sat on top of his desk, open wide and loaded with manila folders. Goff had more of them in hand, and his filing cabinet hung open. A different suit again, Slater noticed. This guy must be living by Agnes's once-a-week rule. Today, however, he looked harried—his tie was loose, his collar button undone.

"Going somewhere, Preston?" Slater asked.

"What do you want?" Goff said, frowning at him.

"Are you clearing out? Does Gil know you're leaving?"

"I'm just going to the mountains for the weekend," he said, affecting nonchalance, but Slater could see that his face was flushed, and his eyes darted around—he was under stress.

Slater closed the door, and was glad to find a deadbolt above the handle. Of course there was a lock: this kind of guy always had a lock. Such a big ego, thinking every woman in the office would fall all over him, so naturally he'd need to be able to lock the door, for all the trysts. Slater turned the knob, the bolt audibly sliding into place.

"What are you doing?" Goff demanded.

"We need to talk," Slater said grimly, moving toward him.

Goff was behind his desk and hefted the duffel bag up by its handles, then set it on the floor as Slater approached.

"Sit down," Slater said, "and keep your hands where I can see them."

"That seems a little melodramatic," Goff said, planting his feet apart and folding his arms.

"Sofía Wallace was here a little while ago."

Goff frowned. "Who?"

"Do not lie to me, Preston," Slater said, raising his voice. "You'll only make me angry. You put her up to sending a chiseler after your boss's daughter. Why?"

"I don't know what you're talking about."

Before Goff could react, Slater grabbed him by the hair and slammed his face into the desk. Goff crumpled into his chair, whimpering and dazed. Blood trickled out of his nose. He put his hands over his face.

Slater waited for him to recover. Pathetic, these suits, thinking they can start trouble for other people without getting any in return. Anyone who'd been slapped around even once would have anticipated that move. This guy was soft, didn't even see it coming—he went down like a rag doll.

"My nose," Goff said finally, still holding it with both hands. "You broke my nose, you *cholo*."

Slater scoffed. "If you think I'm a *cholo*, you don't actually know what a *cholo* is, you racist fuck. Let me see."

Goff recoiled in his chair as Slater reached for him, but he let him pull his hands away from his face, eyeing him suspiciously as Slater gently touched it with his fingertips.

"It's not broken, you big baby." Slater wiped the blood on his hands onto Goff's padded shoulder.

"This is a four-thousand-dollar suit," he protested.

"Really?" Slater said, stepping back and cocking his head, looking him over. "It doesn't fit you that well. I'm thinking maybe you got ripped off."

Goff pulled out his pocket square and dabbed at his nose, then looked at the blood it had absorbed and moaned. "I'm calling the cops."

"Great idea," Slater said, hands on his hips. "I'll be telling them all about your deal with Sofía. Did you know the guy that the pair of you hired shot Agnes up with smack, then tried to blackmail her with photographs of her with a needle in her arm? How do you suppose Gil would feel about you being the cause of that? And how will you explain that to the cops?"

Goff just stared at him, and dabbed his nose again, examining his pocket square.

There was a sharp knock at the door, and the handle rattled. "Preston?" It was Karen Chen's voice. "What's going on in there?"

"Leave us, Karen," Goff shouted. "I'm fine."

"Time to sing, Preston," Slater said quietly. "Sing like a bird, or I really will break your nose."

Goff held up his bloodied palms, gesturing for him to back off. "Nobody was supposed to get blackmailed, or injected with drugs. I just wanted a back-channel to Gil. You know, some leverage with him."

"Why?"

"In case he tried to screw me over—which is obviously happening, if you showed up."

"You think I'm working for Gil?" Slater said, frowning.

"Aren't you?"

"Why did you use Sofía? What's the connection?"

"She's a lowlife, and she knows lots of lowlifes. I certainly don't. I knew she'd have those contacts."

"If you don't know any lowlifes," Slater demanded, "how do you know her?"

Goff checked his nose again to see if it was still bleeding, dabbing with the pocket square. "She's a supplier. She's here all the time."

"She sells cans of soup and root vegetables for the crews on cargo ships," Slater said. "Garbanzo beans too." He watched Goff closely, but saw no reaction. "She has nothing to do with controllers, Preston, or any other kind of electronics. What is she supplying you with?"

Goff blinked rapidly, and Slater could tell he was mentally scrambling. He'd said something he hadn't intended to say, and now he had to lie.

"She provisions the ships that carry our products," he said finally.

"Bullshit. Why is she really here?"

The door rattled and flew open, revealing a portly gray-haired guy in a security guard's uniform, holding a big ring of keys. He wasn't armed, Slater quickly determined. Behind him was Karen Chen, carrying a baseball bat, but holding it in one hand, halfway up, like she had no idea how to use it, for sport or any other purpose. That seemed odd—did she keep that under her desk?

"What did he do to you?" Chen demanded.

"Nothing," Goff said. "I had a small accident."

"You're bleeding," she whined, and then turned to Slater. "You—get out of here, or so help me, I'll split your head open."

Not holding the bat in the middle, you won't, he thought, but raised his hands. "No need to shout, Karen. We're just having a conversation. I was asking Preston about the Indians."

Chen's expression shifted, from anger to alarm. She looked to Goff. "What did you tell him?"

"Nothing," Goff shouted. "Karen, shut up."

She looked back to Slater and brandished the bat. "I said, get out."

Slater could easily disarm her, he knew, but the elderly security guard was looking worried, and he could cause trouble later if he witnessed a scuffle, or worse—if Slater took her bat away, the poor guy might drop dead of a heart attack.

Raising his palms again, he said, "No need for violence, Karen," and gestured toward the doorway, starting toward it and giving her a wide berth. "Most problems can be solved with words, you know. You should look into anger management."

In the doorway, passing the guard and meeting his suspicious gaze, he said, "Such a hothead, that one, am I right?" and trotted down the stairs and out to the street.

ELEVEN

NCE HE WAS in the Thunderbird, he checked the tracking app. Sofía had made another stop, near her business in San Pedro. The minutia of her movements wasn't useful anymore, as he'd already confirmed what he suspected: she was conspiring with Goff. More significant was that the battery on the tracker was down below forty percent. That thing had cost him a lot, and it would be easier to get it back while it was still active, when he knew exactly where it was.

Sitting there for a minute, he thought it through. It felt like the pieces were coming together, although a couple of things didn't make sense. Why was Sofía provisioning a company with only eight employees? Their needs were nothing like those of a cargo ship's crew, out on the sea for weeks at a time. Goff hadn't been lying about how he knew her, but he'd lied to walk it back. And why did the mention of the word *Indians* evoke a reaction from every one of these people, every freaking time? Sofía wasn't going to tell him anything, he knew that, and surveilling her seemed pointless. Still, he wanted the tracker back.

Just as he was about to shift into gear, in the rearview mirror he caught sight of a vehicle pulling into Gislitech's gate—the brown Bentley. It was too soon for Goff to have summoned Martinson because of what Slater had said to him, and if Goff thought Slater was working for Martinson, he wouldn't tell him about it anyway. No, this was nothing to do with Slater, just the boss dropping by the office. He'd wait, he decided, and see where Martinson went.

It didn't take long to find out—less than twenty minutes, by the clock on Slater's phone. The Bentley pulled out of the gate and rolled past him on the street, Max oblivious to his presence, Martinson invisible behind the dark tint of the rear windows. Slater waited until they turned onto the boulevard, then pulled out, racing to catch up. Pulling up at the end of a line of vehicles waiting at a light, he thought he'd lost them, but just for a minute. Up ahead the Bentley turned right, onto the freeway ramp. Slater grinned. The freeway was

Thunderbird home turf, and the way Max drove, he'd have no problem catching up and keeping them in sight.

They weren't headed back to the South Bay, but merged onto the 10 westbound. Slater stayed well back, even though Max wouldn't recognize the Thunderbird, had never seen it. Before long he exited, in a neighborhood where most of the signage was in Chinese—Monterey Park, maybe, or San Gabriel. The Bentley turned into the vast surface parking lot of a sprawling strip mall, and Slater followed, slowing down to see what Max was going to do. Turning into an aisle near the shops, Max pulled into an open space in front of a restaurant. Slater turned in a few aisles farther back. The lot was crowded, probably because of the massive supermarket at the other end, but he found a space and parked, watching the Bentley.

Max stepped out and stood on the curb, waiting for Martinson, who climbed out and joined him. It was interesting that Max hadn't opened the door for him—for some reason he merited more respect than Catalina. Neither spoke as they stood there, scanning their surroundings, and then they both turned, Gil smiling in recognition. Parked a few spaces away was a white Beamer. Why were those damn things always black or white? A man in a dark suit was getting out of it.

Martinson greeted the suit with a handshake.

Slater didn't have a good view, partly blocked by an SUV parked between the Thunderbird and the restaurant, so he grabbed his binoculars, looping the strap around his neck, and stepped out, walking behind the other cars in the aisle and stopping beside a minivan. Once he'd determined it was unoccupied, he positioned himself in its shade, leaning on the vehicle so that he wouldn't be seen, and held his binoculars to his eyes.

Martinson and the suit were talking, with Max standing respectfully a few paces away, suspiciously scanning the parking lot, his hands clasped in front of him like a goddamn bouncer. The only way he could be more obvious about his role was if he put on a sandwich board that said BODYGUARD. The suit had spiky black hair and was probably the same generation as Martinson, and definitely from Asia, Slater thought, based on his body language—erect and formal, bowing from time to time. He'd obviously grown up over there. Martinson put his hand on the man's back, and they walked into the restaurant together, Max trailing behind.

Slater really wanted to hear what they were talking about, but the restaurant didn't look very big. Max was being watchful, so there was no way he could go inside without being spotted. He stood there with the glasses to his eyes, trying to see through the glass in the door into the dark interior. That was his mistake, he'd tell himself later: spending too long with the binoculars, losing track of his immediate surroundings.

"Who are you spying on?" a voice behind him demanded.

Slater spun around, the glasses dropping onto his chest. The guy was young, and wiry, and probably Chinese, based on his heavy accent. Most alarming was his body language—his hands were in the ready stance of a confident martial artist.

"I'm not spying on anybody," Slater said, stepping sideways, so that his back wasn't against the minivan.

"The boss likes his privacy," the guy said, and quick as lightning punched Slater in the face.

Slater knew he was no match for someone skilled in martial arts, and the only outcome of tangling with this guy would be bruises and pain. But one thing he did know was how to get away from a conflict, and he rolled with the punch, ducking and twisting out of striking range.

His assailant was just two steps away, but Slater was in the middle of the aisle now, and as he'd hoped, a car navigating it slowed to a stop, waiting for him to move. That made the martial artist hesitate, not wanting witnesses to the impending beat-down. Slater stood up but held his ground, blocking the car, keeping his eyes on his attacker and touching his upper lip. It was wet, and there was blood on his fingers.

"I'm bleeding, you dumbass," Slater said. "Why would you do that?"

The driver of the car laid on the horn—a gutsy move, Slater thought, considering they were in the middle of an altercation, but he ignored it, waiting for his aggressor to give up and leave. He didn't, waiting for Slater to make a move. Moments later a golf cart rolled up, driven the wrong way up the aisle by a uniformed security guard. It stopped a few feet from Slater. She was unarmed, Slater noted, glancing at the guard as she stepped off the cart.

"What's going on here?" the woman asked, hiking up her belt. "Your nose is bleeding. Did he hit you?"

"No," Slater, said, not looking at her, keeping his eyes on the guy. "I ran into a car door."

"I know you're lying," she said, scowling and looking from one to the other. "You can't be fist-fighting here. This is a family kind of place, not a crack-addled back alley."

"I was just leaving," Slater said. "Maybe you could spend a moment with my friend here while I do that. Ask him about his boss."

"What are the binoculars for?" she demanded, but Slater was already walking past the golf cart toward the Thunderbird. Jumping in, he backed out and left her with the martial artist.

Focus, he told himself, and drove slowly to the

end of the parking lot. That punch had frazzled his thinking, but he was out of danger now, and soon he knew what he had to do. Turning into the aisle where the Bentley was parked, he slowed to a crawl, just long enough to write down the plate number of the white Beamer, then headed for the boulevard.

Once he was a few blocks away, he pulled over and spent a minute examining his nose, pulling the rearview mirror toward him. The bleeding had already stopped, and it didn't seem to be swelling up, although it hurt when he touched it. Cleaning up the dried blood on his lip, he pushed the mirror back into place. It was hard to be mad about getting punched, because he dished out plenty of that himself—it was inevitable that it came back to him once in a while.

There was a great vegan Chinese joint somewhere out here, he knew, and he found it on his phone, happy to see it was just a few minutes away. He found street parking out front, and after he fed the meter, went inside. The host tried to seat him in the window, but he asked if he could sit farther back, out of public view. She let him pick, as the place wasn't busy, and he found a table near the kitchen door.

After he'd ordered, he thought through the encounter with the martial artist. Even though he hadn't been able to listen in on Martinson's meeting, he knew that whoever the suit was, he had a goon working for him who had a lot more skill than Max. Pulling his phone out of his pants, he dialed Conrad's cell, glad that he picked up.

"It's my day off, Slater," he answered, annoyance in his tone. "What do you want?"

"Can you run a plate for me? It's kind of urgent."

"What did I just say?" he demanded. "I'm not at work."

"Maybe you can pause your video game and ask a friend who is working today? All I need is the owner's name—a few seconds of typing on your cop computers. I'm really close to blowing this case wide open."

"No," he said flatly.

"There is the delicate matter of those compromising photos," Slater said.

Conrad laughed. "I think you keep bringing that up because you want people to look at your dick." He was quiet for a moment, then said, "Text me the tag number. I'll see what I can do."

"You're the best, toots," Slater said, and looked at the screen to end the call before he texted him. His food arrived, and he tucked in, but moving his jaw made his nose hurt where he'd been punched, so he had to eat slowly, methodically.

After he'd paid and gone out to the Thunderbird, he checked his phone and saw that Sofía had left her company again, or at least the red dot marking her pickup had. It would definitely be easier to get his tracker back if she parked it somewhere public. On the freeway the afternoon traffic was slowing down, and as he got closer to Long Beach it became stop-and-go. Crawling south, he watched as the red dot moved on the map, traveling fairly fast along the waterfront until she got on the 710, headed north, straight toward him.

Eventually she exited the freeway in the north part of Long Beach, onto a boulevard that he knew was the line separating a tony neighborhood to the south and one just north that had been redlined back in the day. People who looked like Slater wouldn't have been allowed to live south of that street, and even though racial restrictions on real estate hadn't been legal for decades, both neighborhoods, and urban neighborhoods everywhere, still carried the ghosts of that legacy. South of the boulevard was wealthier, with manicured lawns, upscale coffee shops, and glittering brewpubs; north was seedy, gritty, with chain-link fences and junk-food outlets, vacant lots, and run-down storefronts that hadn't been renovated in forty years. Which side was Sofía headed to?

She turned north, finally, into the seedy redlined neighborhood, and the dot stopped on

Atlantic Avenue. Slater was just a few minutes away. Once he was off the freeway, he pulled over to park a block from where Sofía's pickup was. Climbing out of the Thunderbird, he strolled up the street, busy now with Latina moms and their kids grocery-shopping after school. He spotted the pickup—across the street, parked in front of a Chinese restaurant in a gritty 1950s standalone. Sofía was nowhere in sight, but it was the only place she could be.

Slater dashed across the busy street, waiting for a break in the traffic, and walked up on the pickup. Stepping into the street in front of it, he scanned the sidewalk to make sure he wasn't being watched, then reached into the box, running his hand along the side wall as he walked until he felt the tracker. He pulled it off and palmed it, barely breaking his stride, and continued past the next car, then stepped back onto the sidewalk. Standing there for a second, he studied the configuration of Sofía's taillights, committing it to memory in case he decided to follow her.

The restaurant didn't look like the kind of place someone would drive out of their way to eat at. Could it be something about Gislitech? Martinson had just met with a shady Chinese guy with a snippy bodyguard. It wouldn't hurt to wait a few minutes, he decided, to see if she was with someone when she came out, and whether she was acting cagey. At the end of the block he waited for the light and crossed the street again, heading back toward his car. The Thunderbird was too far away to use for surveillance, but there was a little bodega, perfectly situated directly across the street from the Chinese restaurant and Sofía's pickup.

Slater bought a coffee and an apple inside, a food choice that Conrad would approve of, although it was completely pragmatic—apples and plain potato chips were the only vegan snacks on offer. Back on the sidewalk, he propped himself against the front of the shuttered business next door to the bodega, munching on the apple and sipping at the paper cup. He wished he'd worn Agnes's ball cap so he could pull it down over his eyes. Even without it, he didn't look that suspicious or out of place, he knew—people would assume he was killing time, waiting for someone, and he fit right into the local demographic. The pedestrians mostly ignored him, although once in a while some kid would catch his eye, and he'd shoot them a grin.

His phone buzzed in his pocket, and he pulled it out, answering the call when he saw that it was Conrad.

"Your plate is registered to Wai-Wan Trucking," he said, and spelled the name. "It's supposed to be a BMW—one of the big honking pollution-spewing models that they can't even sell in California."

"That's what it was," Slater said.

"The company's in Rosemead. Do you want the street address?"

"No need. I can look it up."

"They also have an address in Calexico."

"Seriously?" Slater said. Calexico was the border crossing where Martinson had scuffled with the feds. That couldn't be a coincidence.

"It's a trucking company, right, so they probably haul stuff from the *maquilas*."

"What's a *maquila*?"

"Those duty-free low-wage factories along the border in Mexico. It's why your shirts cost two dollars, and a crate of processed snack treats costs less than an apple."

"Interesting," Slater said, absorbing it all.

"That alone smells like organized crime to me. You know about Chinese gangsters, right?" Conrad said. "You do not want to mess with those guys."

"I think I kind of already did," Slater said. "Anyway, thanks for your help. I owe you one."

"Many, Slater. You owe me many, many, many."

Slater chuckled and ended the call, then looked up Wai-Wan Trucking. Nothing online specifically implied that the company was connected to the underworld, or even the *maquilas,* but there wasn't much information about it at all, beyond a terse description on a business-to-business website:

> Road transportation of containers from the Port of Los Angeles and across international boundaries.

It was nebulous in the way a gangster would want to be nebulous, Slater decided, but it didn't necessarily mean Wai-Wan was run by gangsters.

The coffee was long gone, the apple core oxidizing in the paper cup at his feet, and Slater had started to think that maybe Sofía really was just eating over there, when he saw a familiar face. It was Max, wearing the same dumpy brown suit, walking up the sidewalk and peering into the shops as he passed. From the look on his face, he was on a mission.

"Hey, Max," Slater said, stepping away from the shop toward the cars parked at the curb. It was a strategic move—if Max was going to attack him, like the martial arts guy had, he didn't want to have his back against a wall.

Max stopped when he heard Slater's voice, and didn't look surprised to see him. There was something in his right hand, but not a firearm, Slater saw with relief. He stopped near the curb, close enough to talk but beyond Slater's reach. There was a big purple bruise under his right eye.

"Did I do that?" Slater asked, tapping his own cheek. "It looks painful."

Max's face contorted into a sneer, and he flicked the object in his hand, which sprang out into an ugly black wand.

"Whoa," Slater said, putting his hands on his hips. "What's with the asp?"

"The what?"

"The asp—the thing you're brandishing right now," he said, pointing at it.

"I thought it was a collapsible baton," Max said, looking down at it and tugging on the end.

"Same thing," Slater said. "Are you going to hit me with it? That would be battery."

"You batteried me, you moron," Max said, glaring at him.

A man and woman walked by, and Max glanced sidelong at them, holding the asp down along his pant leg, out of view. They weren't looking at him anyway, focused on their own animated conversation.

"I was defending myself," Slater said. "You had a shovel, remember? That would have done a lot more damage than your stupid asp."

"You didn't have to give me a black eye."

Slater scoffed. "How did you find me, Max? Were you tailing me?"

It hadn't seemed like that, because Slater had arrived quite a while ago, and Max had come from the opposite direction.

"You don't get to question me, trash bag," Max said.

Slater watched warily as Max lifted the asp, tapping it on his palm. It was a small weapon, less than two feet long, and didn't look that dangerous, but Slater knew it was made of steel and could inflict serious injury. It gave Max an advantage if he wanted to get into it, but most likely Slater would just wind up taking it away from him, embarrassing him again, blackening his other eye. Max's cocky attitude felt abrasive right now, definitely worthy of a beat-down, but there might be more to learn by engaging with him instead.

"I get it," Slater said evenly. "You're upset. Although 'trash bag' is certainly nicer than what you called me last time. My father was from El Salvador, and his people did indeed enjoy beans as a fundamental component of their cuisine. I eat them myself, so in a way, 'beaner' is an accurate description. But I know it was meant as a slur."

Hearing that, Max was blushing a little, maybe—the first cracks Slater had seen in his hard-ass demeanor.

"Seriously, though—how did you find me?" Slater said. "I'm totally impressed that you did. In a city of ten million people, I'm on some random boulevard, and you walked right up to me. You're like a bloodhound."

Max hesitated, fidgeting with the asp, then said, "It's actually kind of cool, the way it happened. Martinson has a contact at a cell phone company. All he had to do was give the guy your phone number, and he sent us a map every time your phone moved into a new cell. Most of them are huge, right, like a mile across, so there was no way to find you, until you came here. There's a microcell right around here, maybe in this convenience store. The map said you had to be within a half block of it. That was a small enough area that I knew I'd find you."

"Fuck me," Slater said. "You knew where I was all day?"

"At one point it looked like you were in Rolling Hills, or nearby. Then your phone was around Gislitech. I dropped by, but you weren't there."

"It's really scary that I can be tracked like that."

Max shrugged. "I don't think an ordinary person could do it. I can't imagine what Martinson had to pay the phone company guy."

"So you're here on Martinson's behalf," Slater said, "rather than to get vengeance for yourself."

"That's right," Max said, straightening up and scowling, as if suddenly remembering Slater was his adversary. "You need to keep your nose out of things that don't concern you."

"Meaning the thing about the Indians," Slater said. "That has to be why you're here. That one little word struck fear into your boss's heart, and everyone else at Gislitech. Do you know what it means?"

He frowned. "I don't know anything about any Indians."

"What about Sofía Wallace?" he asked. "How is she connected to Gislitech?"

"You're not listening," Max said. "The message is, back off, or else."

"Or else what?" Slater demanded.

"Pain," Max said, holding his gaze and raising the asp, then slamming it into the passenger window of the sedan parked beside him at the curb. The glass shattered with a loud *pop*, some of the jagged chunks raining down into the gutter.

"Well, it'll be painful for whoever owns that car," Slater said.

Max stared at him. "That's not your car?"

"I'm parked up the block."

Max's mouth became a tight line, and he pushed the tip of the asp into his palm, struggling to collapse it.

"Use the concrete," Slater said.

Max scowled and leaned down to bang the tip onto the sidewalk, finally breaking the friction grip and sliding it closed. Turning on his heel, he strode up the street. Slater didn't linger either, especially since a couple of people had stepped out of the bodega to see what the noise was. Shrugging at them, he walked back toward his car. Across the street, Sofía's pickup still sat at the curb.

From the driver's seat in the Thunderbird, in the fading daylight, he could just make out her pickup down the block, and decided to wait and see what he could. The binoculars didn't reveal much more, and he kept watch without them until she stepped out of the Chinese restaurant. Even without the glasses Sofía was unmistakable, with the poufy hair and familiar body shape, still clad in black. She was alone, and glanced around the street as she climbed into the pickup.

Slater started the Thunderbird as she rolled by, and pushed his way into the traffic. It took a while to make a U-turn, as the oncoming vehicles were moving fast, and when he finally gunned it and turned left, an oncoming car blasted him with its horn.

Roaring up the street, the pickup's taillights were nowhere to be seen, even though he changed lanes a couple of times, scanning the side streets. It didn't help, and when he got to the freeway ramps, one leading in each direction, he knew he'd lost her.

TWELVE

T HE TRIP HOME was mostly in heavy traffic, and by the time he'd parked, worn out from the slog, he knew he really needed to get off. Opening the fridge, he grabbed the pickle jar and pulled one out, munching on it absently while he stood in the kitchen, staring into space, and then ate another. Stretching out on the sofa, he opened the hookup app and swiped through some of the faces and torsos of guys nearby. A couple of familiar faces popped up, but no one that he wanted right now. He widened the search area and swiped through more, stopping at the head shot of a guy with shaggy hair that had blond streaked into it. He had pale blue eyes and a goofy smile. Slater could definitely handle goofy.

His written profile was brief, culminating with "Total bottom. Make me feel it."

This guy seemed kind of perfect, Slater thought, and messaged him:

> I want to pull your hair and fuck you hard. My place only.

Being so direct sometimes scared guys off, but scared wasn't the type he wanted anyway. Setting his phone on the carpet, Slater rubbed his eyes, feeling tired now. His mind had started to sink into sleep when his phone buzzed with a response from the blond.

> Text me your address, and don't shower.

Thumb-typing the details, Slater grinned to himself, then got up to collect the laundry strewn around his bedroom, dumping it into the bottom of the closet. In the kitchen cupboard he found a mini packet of soda crackers, and ate a couple, washing them down with a short pull from the bourbon bottle. Chewing made his nose hurt, so he went to look at it in the bathroom mirror. It wasn't swollen, and looking inside his nostrils, he couldn't even see the wound. He shook some ibuprofen tablets into his mouth and washed them down with another slug of bourbon.

Soon there was a knock on the door, and he pulled it open to find the blond. He was a little older than his photo, but not to the point that Slater felt misled.

The guy grinned as he stepped inside. "You look like your picture."

"I'm glad."

"What's your name?"

Slater told him, and the blond introduced himself as Bart. He was swishy, his voice melodious, which he hadn't expected. But Slater could appreciate swishy.

"It's an interesting place you've got here," Bart said, stepping into the living room and glancing around.

"Dude—don't even try," Slater said sharply, hands on his hips. "I know it's a dump, and I know it's a shitty neighborhood, and I'm perfectly content with all that."

"OK." Bart nodded, and hesitated for a second, then said, "I never meet guys like you. You're so butch."

"You like that, I'm thinking?" Slater said.

Bart nodded. "I brought handcuffs."

Slater chuckled. "Excellent. I hope you brought the key too."

"I like this shirt, though, so maybe I'll take it off before we go there."

Slater led him to the bedroom and sank onto the futon, leaning back. "Take off your shirt," he barked.

Bart didn't hesitate, pulling the lavender polo shirt over his head. He was skinny, and pasty, definitely not a gym rat. Reaching into his back pocket, he tossed Slater the cuffs.

"These are like cop handcuffs," Slater said, examining them, already getting hard just thinking about putting them on Bart.

"I know, right?" he said, grinning.

"So—do they go on gently," Slater asked, eyeing him, "or are we doing this the hard way?"

Bart's eyes grew wide. "I've been bad, sir—very bad. I think it needs to be rough, don't you?"

Slater stood up and grabbed one of his wrists, twisting him around and wrestling him downward. Bart flopped awkwardly onto the futon. It was amazing, Slater thought, how so many people had no idea how their bodies were going to move when they were manhandled. Bart struggled, and Slater held his thumbs together, deftly clicking on the handcuffs.

Slater flipped him over and got close to him, jutting his chin in his face. "You're not going anywhere."

Bart had a visible hard-on under his khakis, and Slater unbuckled his belt and pulled them off. Back beside him again, he grabbed a fistful of Bart's hair and twisted his head, then kissed him, gently. Bart wasn't very good at it, he realized; he was too eager. But Slater spent time slowing him down, methodically working on his mouth. He reached down and penetrated him with his fingers, making a show of being rough but really being gentle when it mattered, working his way in slowly.

Eventually he couldn't wait any longer, and rolled a condom onto his rock-hard cock, pushing Bart on his side and sliding inside him. Bart was breathing hard, his eyes closed. Slater grabbed his hair again, increasing the tempo of his thrusts.

"You've got me, sir," Bart said. "I can't move."

Pounding harder, through gritted teeth Slater snarled in his ear. "What are you going to do about it, huh? You're soft, you fucking desk jockey. Take it like a man."

Slater came quickly, and stayed inside him, stroking Bart's cock until he came too, arching his back and moaning. He pulled out, finally, and held Bart close, his breathing slowing, one fist on his chest, and started to drift into sleep.

"I wonder if you could unhook me," Bart said, once he'd caught his breath.

"In the morning," Slater said.

Bart didn't reply, didn't move.

"Jesus, man, I'm joking. Where's the stupid key?"

"On my keyring, in my pants," he said.

Slater got up to find it, and unlocked the cuffs. Bart flopped onto his back, rubbing his wrists, relieved.

"Do you want a drink?" Slater asked him. "I've got bourbon."

"No thanks."

He flipped off the light and went out to the kitchen, opening the bourbon on the counter and chugging from the bottle. His throat burned with that best kind of pain. Back in bed, he waited for the golden rush to wash over him.

"You smell like a distillery," Bart said in the dark.

"Thank you," Slater said, covering his eyes with his arm.

———◆———

WAKING IN DARKNESS, SOMETHING warm and hard was pressing against his leg. Looking at the clock, it wasn't even midnight. There was a body connected to that warm cock, he thought, and then remembered.

"Want to go again?" Bart asked.

"I don't think I can. I'm a little buzzed."

"I meant me. Let me fuck you."

"Yeah, I guess," Slater said, and squeezed his woody.

Reaching over to find a condom, Slater rolled it on for him. Bart was trembling like a puppy, so excited about doing this. Slater turned on his back and guided Bart gently as he climbed up. Bart penetrated him all at once, with no preparation, no warning.

"Aw, man," Slater said, groaning and shifting his pelvis.

Bart was either stupid or selfish to do that, but Slater could handle it, focusing on suppressing the pain. Bart pumped intently, moving fast, his arms wrapped around Slater's shoulders. Slater was just getting into it, finally comfortable and appreciating the rhythm, when Bart thrust for a final time, straining and whimpering in ecstasy.

Slater waited patiently for him to pull out, then turned on his side, and was drifting into sleep again when Bart spoke.

"Can I take a shower?"

"I don't think you'll want to, once you see it," Slater said, "but help yourself."

"I'll just go have a look," he said, and got up.

"There's nothing to steal," Slater mumbled.

"You son of a bitch," Bart said, standing at the foot of the bed. "I live in Hancock Park. My mortgage is ten times what your rent is in this shithole. I'm not going to steal from someone like you."

Slater sat up on one elbow, fully awake now. "I've offended you."

"Why would you assume I'm a thief?" he demanded.

"It's the world I work in. There are lots of rough people—it's all I see all day long. I can tell you're from a higher stratum, though, if that helps. Your haircut alone probably cost more than my rent."

Bart chuckled. "Is that why you called me a desk jockey? I'm not, by the way."

"I guess I was thinking about someone else."

"I thought so. You called me 'Preston.'"

Bart padded out, and Slater heard the water go on. He might live in a better neighborhood, but he wasn't too snobby to use that shabby shower.

———◆———

WAKING, SLATER SAW THE glowing numbers of the clock. It was early. He waited for the memories to drop in, as they always did. For now, though, he was content not to have a dry mouth, or feel dehydrated and headachy. Maybe he hadn't drunk anything last night. But then he remembered that he had, just earlier than usual. There'd been a guy too, but he wasn't here now.

Preston, he remembered, in his office, loading up a duffel bag like a damn cat burglar. Karen holding a baseball bat as if she were going to twirl it like a majorette. Max and his stupid asp, which he didn't even know how to use, smashing some random car window. Sofía and her onions and garbanzos. Loose garbanzo beans on the shop floor. Little bits of Chinese plastic, locked doors, and sealed-over windows. Then, suddenly, his mind was clear, and it all made sense—all the pieces clicked into place, and he knew what he had to do.

Pulling on his jeans and a clean shirt, then Agnes's blue ball cap, he spent a minute looking for his satchel, then remembered he'd left it in the trunk of the Thunderbird. It had a serious brick of cash inside, and he hadn't wanted that lying around when he had company. Trotting down to the garage, he found his dark sunglasses in the dash and pulled them on as he backed into the alley.

He navigated to the freeway as quickly as he could, driving hard through downtown and into east LA County. At Gislitech he parked up the street a ways, even though he was impatient to do what he'd come to do, and opened the trunk, lifting the carpet and pulling out a crowbar, its cold heft satisfying in his hand.

The front entrance of the Gislitech building was unlocked, which made sense—it was already business hours. A different woman, in a powder-blue jacket, sat at Karen Chen's desk. She looked alarmed when she spotted the crowbar in Slater's hand, the determination in his gait.

"Can I help you?" she asked timidly, but Slater ignored her, striding to the door that led onto the shop floor. It was locked.

"Open it," he demanded, looking at her.

She shook her head. "I can't do that."

Slater examined the door. It had a simple magnetic lock with no reinforcement. Rather than coerce the receptionist, it would be faster to open it himself. He rammed the straight end of the crowbar into the latch and pulled hard. The door popped open easily, with the loud crunch of splintering wood and the shriek of twisting metal.

Slater kicked it open and walked onto the shop floor. No one was working at the tables, still lined with trays of the little black electronic bits, stacks of flat corrugated boxes at the ready. Striding past them, he headed to the door that led to the upper floors, the door where he'd found the garbanzo beans. This one looked sturdier. He rammed the crowbar into the lock and spent a few seconds reefing on it, back and forth, throwing all his weight into it, until the mechanism finally broke and it popped open with a bang.

A dark stairwell led upward, to a landing and then up another flight. Slater pulled off his sunglasses. Stale humid air washed over him, tainted with the tang of old sweat and cooking, and the idiosyncratic scent of cumin, turmeric, ginger: Indian food. He climbed up two steps at a time, emerging into a room half as large as the shop floor below, but hot, and stuffy, lit only by fluorescent lights, the windows covered over with wallboard. Stepping into the space, Slater stopped short—there were a dozen pairs of eyes on him. They were all men, all South Asian, some in T-shirts, some bare-chested, staring at his intrusion, uncertain. These were the Indians.

They stood between two long tables, jumbled with the same black electronic junk he'd seen being packaged downstairs. This space was more chaotic, though, with piles of the pieces split open, tiny components exposed, and other machinery with wires and gauges. They were assembling them, he realized.

"Do you speak English?" Slater asked, glancing around at the men. They'd all stopped working to watch him.

"Of course we speak English," the man standing closest to him said, his accent thick. He was older than the others, bands of gray streaking his hair.

"What's your name?"

"Houri," he said.

"Are you being held against your will, Houri?"

He glanced at some of the others, but gave no response.

"Where are you sleeping?" Slater asked.

One of the other men, gaunt and with wild hair, pointed upward. Slater sighed. They were being kept here to work, like it was some Third World hell hole.

"Did they take your passports?"

"Yes," Houri said, bobbing his head.

Behind him, Slater heard footsteps, and turned to see Max, in his ugly brown suit, reaching the top of the stairs, breathing heavily from the effort. The lurid black muzzle of a pistol protruded from his hand.

"Drop the weapon, chump," Max said, gesturing with the gun.

Slater hesitated, but then stooped, setting the crowbar on the floor, then rose again, showing his palms at his sides.

"Seriously, with the rod again?" Slater said. "Did you fish that thing out of the pool?"

But Max had seen the others now, the Indians. "Jesus," he muttered under his breath, taking in the scene. His focus shifted back to Slater. "You broke in here with a weapon. I could blast you right now and totally get away with it."

"Maybe if we were alone," Slater said. "With a dozen witnesses to testify that I was unarmed, though, you'd definitely be sent up for murder one. Where's Gil?"

Max nodded to the staircase. "Right behind me."

"Are you sure about that?"

Doubt crept into Max's eyes, and he looked at the Indians again, but caught himself before he looked to the stairs.

"Did you know these people were up here?" Slater asked him intently. "You looked surprised, so I don't think you did." Still holding his palms where Max could see them, Slater turned to Houri. "Have you seen this man before?"

"I've never seen either one of you," Houri said.

"That's such good news," Slater said, turning to Max. "It means that at this moment, Max, you haven't done anything wrong. But if you keep me here, even if you don't shoot me, you're an accessory to whatever this is." He gestured with his head to the men behind him.

"Let's see what Gil has to say," Max said, and shouted toward the stairway, keeping the gun trained on Slater. "Gil—I've secured the room. It's safe to come up."

They listened, but there was only silence.

"Crickets," Slater said. "He bailed. You, however, don't have to be the fall guy for the millionaire. This is your chance to do the right thing. I know you want to, Max. I know you, because I am you."

"*Sang froid,*" Max said, raising an eyebrow.

Slater grinned at him. "Right. Help me fix this. Help me help these guys."

Max watched him for a moment, and Slater saw his eyes flick around the room again. He pulled open his jacket and holstered his weapon.

"The woman on the desk called 911 when

you broke down the door," Max said. "Then she phoned upstairs to Gil. He was furious that she'd already called the cops." He looked away. "I know you're right. He's long gone."

"Where's Goff?" Slater asked.

"He's the reason Gil came in today. Gil hasn't been able to get hold of him since yesterday afternoon. Goff was acting all squirrely then, and he's not here now."

"He was in on this," Slater said, "and he got spooked. He's probably headed for Mexico too."

"Who are these people?" Max asked intently. "What's going on?"

"Something felonious, don't you think? Gil took their passports and hid them up here." Slater looked around at the men, their eyes still on him and Max. "Are you being paid a salary?"

"We're paid maintenance," Houri said.

"What does that mean?"

"Room and board. After we complete our contracts, we get paid."

"But only if we're out of debt," the guy with the wild hair said. "We owe the boss for bringing us here. We have to pay him back for that. I owe him more for the travel expenses than the payment for the one-year contract. I will have to stay to work for another year."

Slater turned to Max. "Does that sound legal? No surprise that Gil isn't hanging around."

"They're like slaves?" Max said, frowning in disbelief.

"Close, but it's done with a contract instead of chains. The result is the same, though—they don't try to run away. It happens a lot in the Middle East. Keep their passports, and tell them they owe you money, so they have to work it off. It's called indentured labor."

"It explains things," Max said, rubbing his forehead. "Several things. The food deliveries."

"Sofía?"

Max nodded. "She'd drop off a pallet of all this food on the shop floor. The next day it would be gone."

"I wonder if she knew about this."

"Why not ask them?"

"Great idea," Slater said, and pulled out his phone. When he'd found Sofía's portrait on her company's website, he stepped over to Houri and showed him. Several of the others crowded around him to look, their reticence evaporating.

"Do you know her?" Slater asked.

Houri smiled. "The food woman."

Slater searched for Gislitech's website and found the photo of Preston Goff, then showed it to them.

"The boss," Houri said, and others murmured agreement.

Swiping to the photo of Gil Martinson, Slater

showed them that as well.

"The big boss."

"They're all in it together," Max said.

"Karen Chen knew about it too," Slater said. "I'm certain of that. When I confronted Sofía, she ran straight to Goff." He put his hand to his head. "Damn it—I know where he is."

In the distance rose the faint sound of a siren, and Max said, "That's the cops."

"That's actually an ambulance," Slater said, "but if that woman called the cops, they won't be long. Can you handle them? I need to go to Goff's office."

"Sure," Max said.

"Where's the boss?" Houri asked.

Slater turned back to him, and looked around at all of them. "The boss and the big boss are both gone. Your contract is finished."

"How do you know this?" Houri asked, frowning.

But the wild-haired guy believed him. "What's going to happen to us now?"

"I don't know, but I wouldn't stay here," Slater said. "The police will be here soon. You can talk to them and ask for help, or you can leave this place and take your chances—but you'll have to do it now, before they get here."

Slater went past Max and hustled down the stairs, along the shop floor, and out to the reception space. The woman he'd seen earlier was gone, and there was no sign of the police yet. Running up the stairs to Goff's office, he found it unlocked. The file cabinet was half open, manila folders and loose paper littering the floor in front of it. Goff had definitely cleared out. Stepping behind the desk, Slater peered at the aircraft photo, and quickly typed the tail number into his phone.

"No cops yet," Max said from the doorway. "What are you doing?"

"Gil might get away, but there's still time to stop Goff. I'm checking to see if he filed a flight plan." It didn't take long to find it, tapping at his screen. "Here it is—today, departing in an hour. KEMT to CYHC. Those are airports, right? Where the fuck is KEMT?"

"You don't have to look it up. Goff keeps his plane at El Monte."

"There's an airport in El Monte?" Slater said, looking up at him.

"A little one. It's twenty minutes from here without traffic."

"Plenty of time to stop him," Slater said, stuffing his phone into his pants and heading toward the door.

"Why not get the cops to do it?" Max said. "They could make one phone call and shut him down."

"You know what they're like. By the time I

explained everything, even if they actually believed it, Goff will be in CYHC, wherever that is."

"Canada," Max said. "Airports that start with C are usually Canadian."

"You're so much smarter than you look," Slater said, and clapped him on the shoulder. "Listen, the cops are going to be out front. Is there a back way out?"

"Through the shop floor, and out the loading dock. There's a vehicle gate onto the alley. It's always chained shut, but there's a door in the gate with a keypad lock." Max recited the four-digit code, and Slater thumb-typed it into his phone.

"What's your phone number, Max?"

He rattled it off, and Slater typed it too.

"Go," Max said, "before everybody gets detained."

Slater hurried down the stairs and caught a glimpse of powder blue—the receptionist, standing in the lobby. He ducked into the shop floor through the broken door.

"There he is," the woman shouted. "That's the guy."

Heart pounding, Slater ran to the loading dock and jumped off, landing in a crouch, then ran across to the back gate. When he typed in the code, the lock snapped open, thankfully, and he scanned the yard as he stepped into the alley, but no one was following him, not yet. He closed the door again to slow them down, then jogged up the alley for a minute, slowing to a walk when he saw no one was behind him.

It was a long, wide alley, typical of an industrial zone, and he cursed when he realized how far it was to the next cross street. When he finally rounded the corner and the Thunderbird came into view, he could see a lone county cop car beyond it, parked in front of Gislitech's office door.

That's why they hadn't followed him on foot—there were only two patrol deputies, which meant they didn't think the receptionist's report about Slater and his crowbar constituted an armed takeover, but something far less significant. That also explained why they hadn't arrived in a rush. Their assessment of the gravity of the day's events would change, however, when they met all the undocumented workers hidden upstairs.

Once he was safely in the Thunderbird, his instinct was to race away, but he forced himself to sit there for the time it took to find the El Monte airport on a map. It was half an hour's drive, if the traffic didn't get worse, his navigation app told him—there was still time.

THIRTEEN

I T DIDN'T LOOK like an airport, driving up on it, but more like a strip mall—a series of small aviation businesses fronted by angle parking. Goff could be in any one of them. He did a U-turn and drove more slowly, reading the names on the signs. He stopped when he found the most likely candidate: Executive Flight Hosting. That would appeal to a bougie desk jockey like Goff.

Slater parked at the curb and walked in the front door. At one side was a counter, and behind it a woman in a dark-blue jacket, but Slater walked past, scanning the rest of the space, which ended with some lounge furniture in front of big windows that looked onto the tarmac.

"Can I help you?" the desk clerk asked, her tone chirpy, but as he walked by, ignoring her, she raised her voice. "Do you have an appointment? Sir?"

There were only two people back by the windows—Goff and a dark-haired woman, standing there looking out at a little jet airplane, familiar from its portrait on Goff's office wall. The woman had her arm around his waist. She laughed audibly, pulling him closer. Slater knew that voice—Karen Chen.

So Goff was walking away from his wife and kids, Slater thought as he strode toward them, the same way he's walking away from a human trafficking rap.

Goff must have sensed Slater's glare and determination, because he turned around to look as he approached. There was a little white bandage on the bridge of his nose, and dark rings under his eyes, which went wide with fear. He held up his palms and backed toward the window.

"Slow down," Goff said. "Let me explain what's going on."

Slater clocked him with a quick uppercut, and Goff spun sideways and crumpled to the floor. It was almost too easy. Karen Chen was screaming now, but Slater tuned her out.

"You can't treat people like trash, Preston," he shouted. "You just can't." Slater kicked him in the stomach, and Goff rolled over, his body jackknifing, hands in his crotch. "Why do you make me do this to you?" Slater demanded. "Why?" He kicked Goff in the kidneys. "Going to Canada? Where then? To enslave more poor people to pay for your jet fuel?"

He was preparing another kick when Chen jumped on his back, beating his head and his chest with her fists. It took him a moment to regain his balance and concentrate on throwing her off, and he stepped away as she tumbled to the carpet. *Enough*, he decided, and backed away from them. He assessed Goff for a second, and then strode toward the front door.

The clerk and several other people were standing around the reception desk, eyeing him fearfully.

"I phoned the police," the clerk called to him, brave now that she was flanked by a couple of burly guys in blue coveralls, one with bright-orange earmuffs around his neck—the ground crew.

"Good," Slater said, pointing back toward Goff, still curled up on the floor, Karen Chen kneeling at his side. "The sheriff's deputies are looking for that man." He stopped and pointed a finger at the desk clerk. "Do not let him leave in that airplane, or I'll make sure you personally get charged with rendering assistance to a fleeing felon."

Walking out the door, he took a deep breath. That probably wasn't even a real crime, but seeding doubt in their minds should slow things down long enough for the cops to get here. Hopefully

Goff was messed up enough that he wouldn't even be able to get on his plane.

In the Thunderbird, he pulled off the ball cap and threw it in the backseat before he drove away.

There was one other bit of business that he needed to make happen today, and he headed home, where he sat in his recliner with his laptop and connected to Cudahy Mutual's servers, logging in and digging around for what he needed. After an hour or so of typing, filling in forms and summarizing his findings, he blew the dust off the laser printer that sat on the floor between the back of the recliner and the kitchen counter, kneeling to connect the cable to his computer and switch it on. It was still working fine, he was happy to discover, despite weeks of disuse.

After he printed all the forms, he separated them into two stacks, stuffing each set into an envelope with a string closure. He found a pen and wrote APPROVE on one envelope and DENY on the other. Both were the same set of forms, but one recommended that Jason Hughes's claim go through, and the other recommended it be rejected. He'd decide which ones he was going to file after he talked to Jason one last time—it all hinged on how much he knew about the Indians.

The drive to Hyde Park went fast, and Slater parked down the block from Jason's over-garage apartment, walking back to it with his satchel over his shoulder. Trotting up the stairs, he knocked on the door, and heard Jason moving around inside. The door opened a crack.

"You," Jason said when he saw him, and tried to close it again.

Slater managed to wedge his boot between the jamb and the door, and Jason gave up, stepping back. Slater pushed the door open but didn't step in.

"Relax, man. I'm not going to hurt you."

"What do you want?" Jason demanded.

"I'm ready to make my final report, and I had a few last questions. Can I come in?"

Jason scoffed and walked into his living room, not limping. Slater took that as a tacit yes, and went in, dropping into the armchair across from the sofa where Jason sat, setting his satchel at his feet. The stench of weed was strong, but it wasn't smoky. Maybe he was vaping it. Why did people think that was undetectable? It smelled almost the same as if it been burned in a joint or in a bong. Jason looked a little buzzed, he decided, softening the edges of his naked hostility.

"I found out what was upstairs from the shop floor at Gislitech," Slater said. "It took me a while, but eventually it all came together."

"Seriously?" Jason said, interested now. "What's up there?"

"You didn't know? The other day you were

afraid to even talk about it."

He gestured helplessly. "I had my suspicions."

"Like what?"

Jason shook his head. "No way. I'm not going to say anything that might piss off Gil and Preston."

"At this very moment," Slater said, "Gislitech is crawling with cops, and Gil is in the wind. I'm pretty sure Goff is going to be behind bars soon. Gil will be too, if they find him. Neither one of them is going to be worried about you at all."

"Huh," Jason said, not looking too surprised, and from his expression, Slater could tell that he believed him. "Was it drugs?"

"What makes you say that?"

"Well, Gil was always going to the border, Tijuana and Calexico, and there were these bulk food deliveries. Gislitech doesn't sell food, right, and nobody works there, so nobody was eating all that. It seemed odd. I thought maybe there were smuggling drugs inside repackaged food."

"Interesting idea," Slater said, and watched him for a moment. Jason didn't seem very bright, especially with the weed-baked drowsy eyes, but Slater couldn't detect any deception—he was telling the truth, and that made his decision easy.

"There were actually people locked up there," Slater said. "At least a dozen of them. All men. Undocumented workers from India."

Jason grimaced in disbelief. "No way. I would have seen them."

"I broke down the door and saw them with my own eyes. They were sleeping up there and working on the electronics, testing them or assembling them or something. They weren't prisoners, except in their own heads, but they couldn't just walk out of there either. He had them all believing they owed him money."

"I knew Gil was up to something shady," Jason said, "but enslaving people? Come on."

"He told me himself that labor was such a pesky input cost. If you eliminate the wage and make people work for food alone, you can cut your salary expenses dramatically. It's the tech industry's wet dream come true."

"It's like the goddamn Middle Ages," Jason said.

Slater scoffed. "Welcome to the glittering new age of technology." He reached into his satchel and pulled out the envelope marked APPROVE. "I need to get this report in today. There's a couple of things you need to sign."

Jason stared at him blankly for a moment, and then his expression shifted as the meaning finally permeated his weed-addled mind. "This is it, huh," he said, leaning forward. "I admit I haven't been entirely truthful—"

"Keep that to yourself," Slater said, cutting

him off. "I'm recommending the company approve your claim." Flipping through the paperwork, he folded it over and handed the sheaf to Jason. "I don't control whether they will—I just advise them on whether I think it's a legitimate claim or not. So I can't promise what the final outcome will be."

Jason took the pages and started reading. Eventually he looked up. "You're saying I really am injured. Why are you doing this? Last week you were spying on me down the street in your car, like I was some kind of crook."

Slater shrugged. "Gislitech turned out to be the real crooks. If they had slave laborers locked upstairs, I can only imagine how they treated you."

Jason nodded. "Do you have a pen?"

Slater pulled one out of his satchel and handed it over. "Make sure you date everything yesterday. If anyone ever asks, that's when we did this."

Scrawling his signature, Jason chuckled. "Gil will be so pissed. His premiums are going to soar."

"I don't think Gislitech is going to survive very long with both principles trying to flee the country. That's why this has to go in today, so that it looks like I finished it before things fell apart."

———•———

SLATER DROVE DOWNTOWN, LEAVING his keys with the valet in the bowels of the skyscraper where Cudahy Mutual had its offices, slinging his satchel over his shoulder and riding the elevator to the thirty-fourth floor. The same stick-thin woman who'd copped an attitude with him on Monday was on the desk, but today she seemed cowed at the sight of him.

"I'm here to see Della," he told her.

"I'll tell her you're here," she said.

"Is there a photocopier I can use first?"

She gestured to the hallway. "In the mail room, around the corner."

Slater grinned at her. "Thanks," he said, and walked where she'd pointed. He photocopied everything Jason had signed and slid the copies into his satchel. There was an industrial shredder in the mail room too, on the floor beside the rack of pigeonholes, so he pulled out the other envelope, the one marked DENY, and ran those pages through, turning them into confetti.

He walked back through the lobby and down the opposite hall toward Della's office, not bothering to check with the receptionist. Della looked up as he came in, and watched as he dropped the sheaf of paper in the inbox on the corner of her desk.

"Jason Hughes?" she asked.

"That's the guy. I wrapped things up with him yesterday."

She leaned back in her chair. "What was your

recommendation?"

"I think he's telling the truth. You should pay him. It's all in my report."

"OK," Della said, raising her eyebrows in surprise. "The actuaries are going to hate you. I bet Gil Martinson will too."

She hadn't heard yet what was happening at Gislitech, Slater realized.

"They shouldn't blame me for reporting the truth. And they can hate me all they want, I guess, as long as I get paid."

She laughed. "When have I ever not paid you?"

"True, but I'm unemployed now. You'll have to send me another case soon."

"You know I always do, Slater, and you know why—you're the best."

FOURTEEN

T HE COPS WANTED to talk to Slater, of course, as he was the one who had busted into the secret sweatshop. The surprising part was that they set the interview at one of the federal buildings, downtown in the Civic Center. On Monday he put on a necktie and a pair of black pants, made of some thin artificial fiber that lacked the sturdy reliability of denim and made him feel half naked.

Slater sat at the end of a long conference table in a sunlit room, and everyone was completely civil; someone even fetched him a coffee. It felt more like a board meeting than an interrogation. A trio of county cops was there, one of them in uniform, but the feds were investigating the immigration angle, and asked him as many questions as the deputies did.

After he'd been quizzed by those agencies, a guy who'd been quiet the whole time spoke up. Wearing an ordinary suit, Slater hadn't figured out who he was, but he looked like a cop, with a little mustache and a brush cut. He said his name was Pérez, and that he worked for the El Monte Police.

"How did you know Preston Goff was going to attempt to flee the country?" he asked.

Slater nodded thoughtfully, and leaned toward the man as he spoke, holding his gaze. If he could make a personal connection, maybe the guy would go easier on him.

"When I dropped by his office on Thursday," Slater said, "he was loading files into a duffel bag. It felt like he was skipping. I didn't figure out why until Friday. The only personal thing on the walls of his office was a photo of his stupid airplane, which stuck in my mind. It seemed like a logical way for him to try to get away. I checked online and found that he'd filed a flight plan for that day."

"He was pretty banged up," Pérez said. "A couple of broken ribs."

"It's unfortunate that happened to him," Slater said. "I went to the airport to ask him to return to Gislitech so that he could answer questions from law enforcement. He and his mistress, Karen Chen, both attacked me. I had no choice but to defend myself."

"That's not how people at the airport described it," Pérez said, frowning. "There were multiple witnesses."

"Does Goff want you to charge me with assault?" Slater asked him.

A woman who'd quizzed him earlier, one of the feds, spoke before Pérez could. "Goff has bigger problems right now."

"Good," Slater said, leaning back. "And you're welcome, for me locating a perp who was trying to flee."

There were more questions, and then statements to sign, different ones for different agencies, and eventually Slater walked out into the late-afternoon heat, feeling like a weight had been lifted from his shoulders, and glad to be done with it.

Just outside the federal building's entrance, sitting on the truck-bomb barrier, which was creatively disguised as a row of concrete benches amid the Southwestern landscaping, was Conrad. He was in his civvies—a light-colored suit, the jacket draped over the bench beside him, and a white shirt with the necktie undone and dangling. Several shirt buttons were open, revealing his chest hair. His eyes were fixed on his phone. Such a beautiful man. He looked up as Slater approached.

"What are you doing here?" Slater said, punching him in the shoulder.

"Ouch," Conrad said, scowling at him and

slipping his phone into his pants. "I heard you were over here. I thought I'd ask how it went." He gave Slater the once-over. "I don't think I've ever seen you wear a tie before."

"So you're stalking me now, is that the way it is? You big freak."

Conrad scoffed.

"You're dressed for court," Slater said.

"That's why I'm down here. So you made your statement?"

"Statements, plural," Slater said. "Everybody wanted one." He looked over his shoulder, then said quietly, "The best news is that they're not going to pop me for battery. I had to slow down one of the knuckleheads at the airport in El Monte, and there was an audience."

"I'm glad. Jail blue wouldn't complement your rich skin tones. So how did the wage-theft sweat-shop thing relate to your insurance fraud case?"

"No connection, as it turns out." Slater watched him for a moment, trying not to look hungry, or worse, sad.

"Do you want to get dinner, maybe tell me about it?"

"I can't. I've got a date."

"Right," Conrad said, nodding thoughtfully. "Your left hand and a bottle of lube."

"At least they make me come," Slater said. "You never did."

"Oh!" he said, laughing. "Slander and lies."

"I have to go," Slater said, even though he didn't want to.

"Have fun."

Slater shot him a wan smile. "Fuck you, Conrad," he said wistfully.

"Back at you," Conrad called after him.

Dive bars were a dying species in this part of town, but Slater knew one nearby, and walked the few blocks over there, loosening his tie on the way. Stepping in the door, he breathed in the sweet scent of alcohol and its by-products evaporating through the skin of generations of sweaty patrons. It wasn't crowded, probably because it was broad daylight and most office workers were still behind their desks, and it was way too early for the hip youngsters who came for the atmosphere.

But Max was already here, sitting at the bar, with a bottle in front of him. It felt good to have someone to talk to who knew what was going on. Slater didn't really have friends that he didn't also fuck, and Max wasn't someone he wanted to sleep with. Slater greeted him and slid onto the next stool.

"How did it go?" Max asked him.

His shiner was starting to fade from purple to yellow, but Slater thought better of mentioning it. "I told them almost the whole truth, and signed off on it. I'm glad it's over."

"The feds had a lot to ask me about Gil. I was in there most of the day."

The bartender stepped over, and Slater said to him, "Double bourbon. Whatever's cheap."

"They didn't actually say it," Max continued, "but I'm pretty sure they don't know where he is. There were lots of questions about the places he used to go overseas, and whether I'd ever overheard anything about stuff he owns in other countries."

"If he stashed money abroad," Slater said, "they'll never see him again."

"They did get Goff, though, thanks to you. He's right up the street in the federal jail."

"I'm just glad I finally got to clock him."

The bartender dropped Slater's bourbon and waited for him to pull a twenty out of his pants, walking away with it to make change. Max raised his beer bottle and said "Cheers."

"Not yet," Slater said, and pulled out his phone, glancing at it. "Three more minutes."

"What happens then?"

"It'll be five o'clock. It's one of my rules. I don't drink more than one before five."

Max chuckled. "So if you only drink after five, that means you don't have a drinking problem?"

"Something like that."

"Right on," Max said, sipping at his beer. "So I'm basically unemployed now. How do I get to do your job?"

"You don't want to do what I do. There's no regular income—half the time I'm waiting around for work. You have a weapons permit, so you have way more options. Sign up with a security firm and be a plainclothes bodyguard."

"I guess that's my plan. I'm not in love with the idea of babysitting airheads like Agnes Martinson."

Slater laughed. "She's not so bad. She gave me that ball cap. I hope she's OK, what with Daddy on the lam."

"More than OK. Her assets have been separate from her dad's since she turned eighteen, so she won't be wanting for anything." He eyed Slater. "So why don't you have a weapons permit?"

"That's a long story."

"Right," Max said, looking away.

"Look at that," Slater said. "It's after five." He raised his shot glass. "Cheers, buddy."